SERVICED

LITTLE BLACK BOOK CLUB

REMI RICHLAND

Talura

I said your name
right – remember
that.

Remi
Richland

COPYRIGHT

Sign up for Remi's newsletter HERE

Follow Remi on Facebook HERE

ONE

MY FEET HURT. My head hurt. My suit jacket felt more like a straitjacket than professional outerwear and I was pretty sure if I were to take it off there would be boob sweat marks all over my cream colored blouse. The heat in Las Vegas was a stifling ninety degrees and it was only eleven thirty in the morning. I still had probably another seven hours of running around to do for the event taking place in ballroom B and I had already been there since seven thirty in the morning. I was damned tired.

My caffeine tank was also running on empty. There were eighteen hotel floors between where I was standing and the coffee shop downstairs, but if I thought I could take the elevator down in any kind of timely manner I was sadly mistaken.

"Miss Beckett, I have an issue with the linen

delivery." The dour-faced head housekeeper, who looked much older than the twenty-eight years I happened to know she was, hurried down the hall as soon as she saw me leaving the ballroom.

"Yes, Lisa, what's going on?" I asked without even slowing. Stopping was a death sentence and only invited more people to congregate. If I stopped moving it gave my feet time to swell in my sensible beige pumps which was unacceptable as I had a lot more walking to do today. If Lisa needed to talk to me, she could talk and walk.

"The linens were delivered, but the table coverings for the Jensen reception are supposed to be blush pink, and these ones are mauve. They aren't just a little off, the packaging is labeled differently as well." Lisa pulled at the corner of her uniform, clearly distraught. I had no idea why she was telling me this, why didn't she just handle it?

"Why did we accept the delivery? You should have just told them to take them back." It was like talking to a small child. Lisa had been here for long enough, it wasn't like this was her first wedding reception, and the Wellsborough Hotel attracted affluent guests. They were paying good money for blush colored linens and they would damn well get them.

"Yeah, well the boxes were labeled blush, the inner wraps were labeled mauve. We didn't notice until they had already unloaded the truck. The reception is tomorrow, what are we going to do?"

The only option we had available —get it taken care of. Sticking to my no stopping rule, I pulled my phone out of my pocket and smashed the button that had the linen company on speed dial. "Jerry Lynn, it's Elizabeth from the Wellsborough. Yes, well not so good," I said in response to her well-intentioned inquiry about how my day was going. "Looks like the driver just dropped off the linens for the Jensen reception tomorrow and they are the wrong color." I paused, listened to her hem and haw for a minute and then cut her off mid-sentence. "It's only been about fifteen minutes since he left, so I would imagine he is at his next delivery location, which, in all honesty, could be anywhere in the local vicinity considering how many hotels there are in the area." We weren't in the heart of Las Vegas, but there was more to the city than just the strip and many other businesses besides the famous casinos. Not everyone's idea of a Vegas getaway had anything to do with gambling. I know mine didn't.

"Well, I figure we have two options Jerry Lynn. You can have him turn around and pick up the incorrect table linens right now, or you can have him go straight back to your warehouse, pick up the right ones, and we can make the switch out when he comes back. Which will be today, am I correct?"

Yeah, I got it was a Friday, an incredibly busy day for anyone in the service industry, especially people like us who were always preparing for the significant events of others, but this was roughly five thousand dollars' worth of tablecloths we were talking about. Fix it.

"Thanks, Jerry Lynn," I said as I ended the call at the same time as I approached the elevators, Lisa hot on my heels. "Go downstairs to the receiving area and tell the boys to get those linens boxed up on the dock. He'll be back in less than two hours to pick them up and drop off the blush." Lisa smiled and a look of relief spilled over her face, "Thanks Miss Beckett, I don't know how you do it. When I call I can't get them to help me out at all."

It wasn't like I was any better at talking to people than she was. I just knew who to call, and had the joy of having the words *Event Coordinator*, after my name is all. People respected the job title, and I had the right phone numbers on speed dial. If Elizabeth Beckett was on the line, money was being made or lost. Regardless, the call needed to be answered. That was all there was to it.

I barely had time to smile and say "You're welcome" before the elevator beeped and the down arrow blinked red. *Yes, timed it out perfectly.* Just eighteen downward lurches between me and caffeinated bliss. Except the elevator didn't lurch down. It lurched upwards. Twice. *Sonofabitch.* I love my job, I really do, but these elevators can take a flying leap for real. I cursed that lying down arrow silently, as I waited for the elevator to stop moving. Since there were two floors of banquet and event rooms in this hotel, located on the eighteenth and nineteenth floor, there were also another six floors of guest rooms. If anyone hits the down arrow on the elevator from any of those upper floors, the elevator will stop its downward trek to go up and pick them up. It was how they eliminated people being stuck on the upper levels waiting for the lower floors to get off and on the elevator. I may have hit the down button, but someone else above me did as well, so in elevator speak that meant I was a second-class citizen for this ride.

Damn it.

The lurching stopped on the twenty-first floor, and I pasted on my most courteous customer service smile as the doors slid open and I shifted my weight slightly from foot to foot. Getting on the elevator meant I had to stop moving and my feet were aching up a storm. I knew better than to wear new shoes on a heavy work day, but they were also super cute and on sale. I had to break them in somehow.

I smelled him before I saw him.

Elevator etiquette dictates that whoever is waiting to exit the elevator has the right of way before anyone entering the elevator, and this person must have known it because there was the span of several heartbeats before he joined me. And *oh* but he smelled divine.

The scent wasn't too strong, more of a subtle change in the air. It was spicy, it was woodsy, and it was....something exotic. If I had been walking out in public and smelled this scent I would definitely turn my head to locate the source. When I saw to whom that enticing aroma belonged to my tongue glued to the roof of my mouth and my polite customer service smile froze on my face.

Silver fox.

There wasn't another phrase I could come up with to describe that man standing next to me. He held himself well, perfect posture in charcoal grey slacks and pinstriped dress shirt with the cuffs rolled up to three-quarter length. Dark hair dusted his arms, the same color that streaked across his temples but the rest of the hair on his head was a glorious silver. Strong jaw, dark brows and even darker eyes comprised a truly awe-inspiring air of elegance and authority. I felt myself lowering my eyes as heat bloomed in my cheeks. The elevator wall pressed against my back and I used it to ground myself in the present. Just because this guy was ripped right from the recesses of my fantasies didn't mean I needed to make an ass out of myself in the elevator. But *good night*, men this attractive didn't just end up next to me in close quarters. I mean, as an event coordinator I worked with a lot of people in the general public, but this man was physical perfection. Men like him didn't exist outside of the books and movies - they just didn't.

It took me a moment to realize that the elevator door had closed but we hadn't moved yet. I observed the man who was looking back at me with a small smile on his face, like I had done something amusing but I didn't know what yet. The elevator should have moved though, so I checked to see if any of the floor buttons were lit up. The ground floor button was blinking.

Wait, that wasn't right. The buttons either lit up

when you pushed them or they didn't, they didn't blink. Something was wrong. I frowned at the button and pushed it again, it continued to blink lazily, like a turn signal that someone had forgotten to turn off when they merged onto the highway and kept driving like that in the hammer lane to the irritation of everyone behind them.

"Is something wrong?" A low voice asked beside me. Wrong? What could be wrong when the sound of his words melted into my skin like butter? Heat flashed across my collarbone and I felt myself drawing the edges of my short sleeved blazer together, making sure I was covered and that the tips of my nipples, which had hardened with desire as soon as I saw him enter the elevator, weren't in view.

Jesus Elizabeth, you're a professional. I was thirty-six years old, not a horny teenager. *Get a grip.*

"No, nothing's wrong," I stammered and immediately felt like an idiot. "Well, something *is* wrong with the elevator, but I know how to fix it," I said, finding my voice and pulling my cell phone back out of my blazer pocket.

"Oh? And how would you know that?" He asked, one perfect brow arched in amusement.

"Magic," and I winked at him. I fucking winked at him, what a dork. Flirting with someone way out of my league in an elevator. Flirting with a guest no less. It was like all of my professionalism flew right out the door as soon as I saw a handsome face. I needed a day off or a vacation. Probably I needed to get laid.

Most likely it was all of the above.

But it wasn't magic that was going to get the elevator moving, it was the power of a phone call, as per usual. Punching in another number on speed dial I actually had to wait for three rings until someone answered.

"Hey, Lizzie, what's going on? You never call me anymore, I've been so lost without you." Blake, the head of hotel maintenance answered the phone in his usual cheeky manner. Blake was always good for a smile or a laugh, and honestly, sometimes I lived for a quick quip from him to get me through those long and tiresome event days, but I didn't have the luxury of joking around. I was in an elevator with a guest. An elevator that wasn't moving. And even though I could have stood in there basking in his unique scent, I highly suspected he had better things to do than hang out with a harried hotel employee.

"Blake the elevator is being...temperamental." I had to choose my words carefully. I couldn't say "Blake the elevator is fucking up again," because that would lead the guest to think that this was a chronic issue, and that was no good. Even though this had, in fact, happened several times before. Not with me in it, but other guests. I was pretty sure Blake knew what to do.

"Which elevator?"

"Um, the one I'm on?" I said, confused. We had four elevators, but I didn't know specifically how he told them apart. "The one that is currently stuck on the twenty-first floor and not going anywhere."

"Yeah, ok," Blake said, and I heard him moving around, probably in his shop near the security office. I heard wheels creaking and groaning and assumed he'd sat down in his chair by his computer. He may have been the facilities manager, which was mainly maintenance, but a lot of his job was surprisingly high tech. A few click-clacks on a keyboard later and Blake had found us, "I'm gonna turn on the eyes in there, make sure you're decent."

"Oh my God Blake you are ridiculous," but I couldn't help laughing. Blake knew how to get a grin out of anyone, especially me. One of my favorite parts of the job was Blake and his easy smile. It didn't hurt that he was easy to look at and incredibly smart. He was the type of guy I could see myself dating if I ever had time for such things. Which I didn't. That and Blake had charisma, and that meant *everyone* liked Blake. I certainly didn't have what it took to compete in a race with so many participants, so I didn't. Blake and I were fine as friends, and if I wondered if he was as good with his hands in other ways besides his job well...what I thought in my head in my free time was my own business, wasn't it?

Besides, right now I was stuck in the elevator with a guest, and there was no sense in thinking idle thoughts about Blake when what I needed to be doing was taking control of the situation and make sure the guest remained calm. I smiled at him while waiting for Blake's next move, but he didn't look upset at all, just smiled politely at me while lounging against the elevator wall.

"I've got my eyes on you right now," Blake came back on the line, this time sounding triumphant. I waved to the security camera tucked into the back corner of the elevator ceiling. "My, aren't you looking ravishing as always."

I snorted with laughter at his overly done shtick. "Blake you are something else. Now that you pinpointed our location," I said in a fake militant tone, "What do you need to get us operational again?"

"I can see the issue right now, and it's actually

not a malfunction on our part, which is a little frustrating. It's the alarm company. Looks like there was a blip in the fire line and it triggered a silent alarm. I just need to call the security company and get them to do a reset. It's simple, but because of protocol it's going to take a few minutes. Five tops, can you hang for a bit?"

Five minutes alone in the elevator with the handsome stranger who smelled like heaven? Oh, the hardship.

"Yeah, we are good in here Blake, you do what you need to do. Thanks."

"You got it, Lizzie. You look pretty today, I like your shoes." Then the line went dead and Blake was off, presumably dialing up the security company with his password so they could do an automatic reset.

I looked up at the stranger who had been waiting so patiently, "I'm so sorry, but Blake is taking care of it. He's our facilities manager here at the hotel and he knows exactly what to do. There's nothing wrong with the elevator, just a mixed signal to our security company, and when that happens the elevator gets an electronic signal to shut down. He's calling for a reset, it should only take a few minutes. I am so sorry for your delay," I apologized again, not knowing

what else I could do except shoulder the respon-
sibility.

"You work at the hotel?" the man asked, looking
surprised.

"Oh yes, I'm Elizabeth Beckett, I'm the event
coordinator here at the Wellsborough," and I
reached my hand out for a shake. But instead of
grasping it like I expected, he slipped his hand
under my own and brought it up to his mouth.
Placing what I am sure was a very chaste kiss on top
of my hand, but set fire to under-utilized libido, he
smiled charmingly.

"I'm Wesley, lovely to meet you. Since you are the
event coordinator, would I have you to thank for the
lovely gift basket of stationary and wine in my room
upstairs?"

Basket of stationary? I did have guests staying at
the hotel that belonged to a particular group that
was having a gathering over the next few days. What
were they called again? The Little Black Book Club?
I had assumed they would be a bunch of little old
ladies, not someone who looked like he stepped off
the cover of GQ – Silver Daddies addition.

"Yes, that was my idea," I said, pleased that he
would take notice. "Honestly I usually try to orga-
nize the baskets in a theme for our special guests,

but I couldn't find anything about your group on the internet, so I didn't have much to go on besides "book club," hence the stationary. Forgive me for being curious, but what exactly is the Little Black Book Club?"

I don't know why I asked. Maybe I was just trying to make conversation while we waited for Blake to fix the elevator, but his eyes practically sparkled with delight as he pulled a card out of his pocket and handed it to me.

"The Little Black Book Club, Ms. Beckett, is not a club, but a service." The warmth of his hand left a tingling sensation on my skin as he slid the card into mine. *I wonder if my hands are going to smell delicious now.* I thought idly to myself while turning over the black card with white lettering and reading the text.

Your fantasy is our specialty. Tell us what you need.

There was a logo, and a website, which utilized the letters LBBC instead of spelled out words, which could be why I couldn't find it when I looked, and no other information. Your fantasy? Oh!

Oh.

"Like an escort service?" I asked, trying to understand. This was Las Vegas, there were a lot of those around and they weren't anything special. Some were downright dirty and essentially just a polite way to advertise prostitution.

"Hmm, maybe, if that was what you needed," Wesley said thoughtfully. "But we are so much more than that. An escort service merely provides company. Little Black Book Club provides a service for people who would otherwise maybe not have the means or the courage to ask for it."

A little shiver ran up my spine at the word *courage*. That could cover a lot of ground.

"That's interesting," I said noncommittally as I placed the card in the back of my phone case, where I would probably forget about it.

"Oh, you would be surprised how interesting it can be. Our company is very creative with our services, and we have a very high approval rating with our clientele. I would love for you to check us out sometime. I'm sure there is something you've been yearning for, Ms. Beckett, if you think hard enough you could come up with something for us."

I laughed then, even though he hadn't said anything funny. "Oh Wesley, I don't have time to think about anything but work," I said once my laughter had calmed down. "I am sure I could come up with something interesting too, but I'm so busy that all I can think to do at the end of the day is take my shoes off and have a quiet moment to myself before I have to go to sleep, get up and do it all again. I love my job, but it's all-encompassing. It's hard to be the one in charge, you know?"

Wesley's eyes changed then, no longer merely polite and smiling, like moments before. Now they held a calculated gleam that changed the atmosphere of the elevator a little bit. Another shiver ran up my spine as he spoke again. "I *absolutely* know where you are coming from. It's so hard when you have to be in control of everything, sometimes it would just be nice to let go, and have someone else do all the work – wouldn't it?"

"Now there's a fantasy," I joked and smiled. This time he smiled back. A slightly friendlier smile than the polite one I had gotten earlier, like we had just shared a secret and were a little more connected. Something just between the two of us. The elevator lurched then and began its slow downward descent. "Blake saves the day," I whispered under my breath, and I was pretty sure I heard Wesley chuckle warmly to himself. As the elevator dinged a few moments later, signaling our arrival on the first floor, he turned to me again. "It was lovely to meet you, Ms. Beckett, I do hope to run into you again."

Wouldn't that be nice? I thought to myself. But

unless he needed services from this hotel again, it probably wasn't likely. It was all work, all the time, for me. He turned left out of the elevator and towards the front door of the lobby. I went straight and made a beeline for the coffee shop at the other end of the first floor.

Give me the caffeine so I can get through another busy day.

It's hard to be the one in charge.

TWO

THE JENSEN RECEPTION WAS A DISASTER, and it had nothing to do with the blush tablecloths or the impeccable decorating done by our staff. Everything the hotel was responsible for went off without a hitch, from the champagne fountain to the tiny glass pebbles etched with the couple's wedding date that were scattered across the tables as decorations and wedding favors. I always prefer a wedding favor that has some sort of function, but whatever, it wasn't my show. No, the real party buster was when the groom's pregnant girlfriend showed up to cause a scene and a huge fight broke out between the groom and the father of the bride.

There was punching, lots of broken hotel property, and forced evacuation of the ballroom. Also, I'd had to call the police because the bride tried to choke the girlfriend, and even if it was one of the trashiest Springer moments this hotel had ever been privy to, you can't just go around putting your hands on a pregnant woman. My heart broke for the bride, but I was also pissed as hell. Our staff had worked their asses off for that reception, I had worked my ass off for that reception, and they treated our hotel like a garbage pit. So much time effort and money had been wasted on a marriage that was built on a lie, and quite possibly one that was ending after only one day.

Relationships were difficult, and it was occasions like this one that led me to believe I was probably better off alone.

Regardless, that party was the last straw and I needed a break. There was no way I could take time off on a weekend, not when there were so many events scheduled. I had a very capable staff, but just like Lisa had proved with the linen incident, some-times things just had to be handled by the boss. And no matter how stressed out and crazy it made me, I was the boss. So on Sunday, I made the executive decision that I would be taking a mini staycation.

Three whole days off, effective Monday.

Ok, it was a tiny thing, but my staff was aghast. I never took time off. Even if I was sick, I had my cell phone next to my bed and my laptop on my lap. I didn't need to stand up and walk around to make phone calls and emails. Shit still needed to get done. But this time, when I told everyone I was going to be out of the office, I specified that I was going to be unavailable. Completely. No phone calls, no emails, nothing. Everything that needed to be done during the week was all standard prep work, nothing they couldn't handle. I would be back on Thursday to help take care of anything that needed to be finished up before the weekend. I was going to have some me time.

I was sitting in my office chair with my head hanging back against the headrest, stretching out my lower back when I heard a knock on the doorframe of my office. The door was open like it always was, but the only person who ever even pretending like they were asking permission to enter my sanctuary was Blake. He always asked first, never just came barreling in with questions or wants. Not that I would mind if he did – but that wasn't Blake.

"Lizzie, you look like a mess," Blake exclaimed, concern showing on his face.

"Thanks for that," I raised one eyebrow to express my sarcasm. Blake looked fresh as ever, sturdy jeans and work boots with his black polo shirt that had the hotel logo on the front. It wasn't right that he should look so sexy dressed down, but I could barely keep my shit together in a professional blouse and skirt set.

"Why do you always look so put together?" I asked, really wanting to know the answer.

Blake's eyebrows practically jumped from his forehead he was so surprised. "I'm not sure what you mean, but if you are telling me you find me wildly attractive then I'll take the compliment." His blue eyes twinkled as he grinned, his dark hair wavy as unruly as always. I could see why all of the women on staff, and even some of the men, lost their heads around him. He was charming as hell, and I don't even think he was trying. I think he just woke up that way.

"I mean why do you always look like you got a solid eight hours of sleep, took a multivitamin and had a healthy breakfast?" I asked, smiling at his words in spite of myself. "It's not fair Blake, you glow. I want to glow too." Okay, maybe I was pouting a little bit, but I'd pulled a muscle in my neck, my shoulders and my feet ached, and I hadn't eaten anything since yesterday afternoon which was a pack of cookies from the coffee shop in the lobby. I'd been too tired when I got home the night before to do anything but faceplant in the bed and this morning had just been so busy with me trying to wrap everything up and order replacement banquet tables and chairs.

I would be billing the Jensen's for that, of course.

"I think you look lovely just the way you are, but you do look extra tired. Are you eating right? What did you eat today?"

"Don't ask, Blake, you won't like the answer." I laughed then, because he still had a look of concern on his face. *Did I really look that much of a mess?* "Seriously though Blake, what's your secret?"

"Self-care." He said as he stepped into the room and plopped down on a chair in front of me and leaned forward, resting his elbows on his legs. "I do take a multivitamin. I also eat well, and I get plenty of exercise. A couple of days a week in the gym will give you an energy boost I promise."

"Um, Blake, did you just tell me I need to work out?" Jesus, what an ego blow.

"No, I just told you what I do to maintain my healthy glow," and then he winked. "You are perfect as you are, but you definitely need to get more sleep.

"Mhm, what's with the stubble then?" I asked, motioning to his chin, which was sporting a dark shadow. In all honestly it was sexy as hell, but definitely not something I remember him wearing before. He was always clean shaven.

"Oh, this?" He asked as he rubbed his jaw thoughtfully. I'm just trying something new. You like it? I heard the ladies go wild for a little five o clock shadow."

"I bet they do," I murmured low, and I saw a shadow cross his face and felt bad, like maybe I had hurt his feelings. That wasn't right though, Blake was loved by everyone. There were plenty of women to stroke his ego on a daily—no hourly—basis.

I stretched again, this time really feeling that pull in the side of my neck, and I rubbed at the sore spot, wincing a bit at the tenderness there.

"What's wrong, did you pull something?"

"Yeah, it got wild at the Jensen party last night. I had to bring out my A game." I chuckled, but Blake's normally smiling face was serious.

"Want me to see if I can rub it out?" He said, his blue eyes warm with concern.

Rub it out? Did he just say rub it out?

My mind went to a very inappropriate place with that question, and even though that wasn't what he meant by those words, my mind definitely pictured him doing something different. Most likely with fewer clothes on. I wondered, not for the first time, just what Blake was hiding under his work jeans and polo. Inappropriate indeed – I was so depraved.

"No offense Blake, but if you touch me right now I won't be able to function for the rest of the day."

He didn't say anything, just looked at me with that piercing stare, eyes boring into me like he was trying to figure out what I just said. And then it occurred to me.

Double entendre.

"Oh God Blake, I wasn't being inappropriate I promise. Holy shit I'm sorry," I said, and I felt my face heating up with embarrassment. "I just meant I can't relax right now, and if you were to give me a shoulder massage I would probably fall asleep in my chair. I still have things to do, I can't relax yet."

"I don't think you've ever relaxed a day in your whole life," Blake said, and his sunny smile was back on his face, his voice whiskey warm and friendly. *Thank goodness*, I thought to myself. *That was almost sexual harassment.* The last thing I needed was for Blake to think I was a pervert. I really looked forward to seeing him every day, I didn't want to make our relationship strained because I made it weird.

"Well I'm about to," I said and leaned towards him like I was letting him in on a secret. "Tomorrow starts my mini staycation. I'm taking three whole days off. In a row." I emphasized, and his eyes widened in shock.

"You rebellious young thing, you. Nice, Lizzie, I'm so proud." Blake dashed away imaginary tears of pride, like a parent at their child's high school graduation. "What are you going to do?"

"I have no idea, Blake. It was a snap decision. But I need some me time, you are right, I haven't been taking care of myself." My eyes snapped wide as I had an idea. "I know, maybe I'll get a massage, a full body one. And a pedicure, and eat three entire well-balanced meals each day. Maybe I'll drink too much wine and hang out by the pool at my apartment complex and hit on all the much younger men. Maybe I'll become a cougar."

Blake laughed loudly then, and I let the sound wash over me in the confines of my small office. Blake's laughter, it was such a pleasant sound. He just had a knack for making people feel relaxed, it was easy being around him. I didn't have to try so hard – I didn't need to be the boss.

"I would like to see you do that, Miss Cougar. But I'll be happy if you get some rest and relaxation." Blake stretched his large body out in the chair before standing and paused before he walked all the way out the door, presumably to go back to work. "It sure is going to be lonely around here without you. Three whole days?" And then he was gone.

Three days wasn't very long, but I bet I could cram it full of awesome things to do.

THREE

I WAS QUITE POSSIBLY the most boring person on the planet. I woke up Monday morning and made coffee like I always did. I spent the rest of the morning cleaning the apartment and organizing the clutter that had accumulated since the last time I had the time to clean. I couldn't start my relaxing in a messy environment, could I?

I took a shower, shaved...everything that needed to be shaved, I exfoliated and then moisturized. I felt squeaky clean, but that was about it. So much for pampering. I thought about giving myself a pedicure, but it seemed like a lot of effort, especially since I needed to go grocery shopping. I did buy several bottles of wine while I was out, but by the time I got home with the groceries, I was too tired to make dinner, much less drink any wine. So I sat in my clean apartment, with the fully stocked kitchen and lamented how lame I had become while I microwaved the spring rolls I had picked up as an impulse buy.

I don't know at what point I became so uninteresting – probably around the time I decided that a career in event planning was my gig and I took a job as an assistant at the hotel, right out of college. There was zero work to life balance in my world, but I managed to work my way to the top, and our event services at the hotel were high ranking and very well received. I made my hotel a lot of money, and they paid me quite well in return. All the money in the world doesn't matter if you don't have the time to spend it. Or you have no one to spend any time with if you had it. It was true – I was lonely. I couldn't even remember the last time I had gone out with my girlfriends. Most of them worked standard nine to five jobs. The weekends were their downtime, and my busiest.

And I was young yet. Barely thirty-six years old, I wasn't out of the race. My breasts were still firm and high, I took care of my skin and had a great complexion. I kept my long dark hair shiny and manageable, and I did look younger than I was, and I knew it. People told me that all the time. A lot of good it did be being in my thirties, looking late twenties, but coming home and passing out in front of the television like someone in their seventies. Forget that, there were people in their seventies who had more active social lives that I did. I would be lucky to be in my seventies.

Staycation day one and I had done nothing but chores. *Hoo-ray*. And I was still tired. I thought back to my conversation with Wesley in the elevator. About how my fantasy would be to have nothing to do, to not be in charge and have someone else take care of everything for a change. It sounded too good to be true, but I had to admit I was just a little bit curious as to what the Little Black Book Club actually did if it wasn't quite an escort service.

I pulled the card out of my phone case and looked at the website on the back, it wouldn't hurt to just look them up. It wasn't like I was signing up for anything. Just a little peek to see what the company that foxy older man worked for. It certainly seemed mysterious.

I clicked the website and was taken to a homepage that looked remarkably like the business card. Simple. Plain. Dark background with small white text in the center of the page. *Discretion is our busi-*

ness. Anonymity is our specialty. What is your fantasy?
What do you desire?

There was a small box underneath the text that said you must be eighteen or older to gain access to the website, and it made me put my birthdate in to continue. It seemed a little weak for security, I mean anyone could type a fake date in. Maybe they just thought anyone younger wouldn't even know about the website. I mean, I had never even heard about it until the group booked a conference room for a day at the hotel. And even after I had the name I couldn't get any information with a web search. It really did seem to be a word of mouth type of thing, they certainly didn't advertise. Oh well, I simply satisfied my curiosity, it wasn't like I had to give them any personal information. I wouldn't give a credit card number or anything like that. I just wanted to see what they were about.

Apparently, that thing about discretion and anonymity only went one way, because I had to fill out about fifty pages of personal descriptions, likes and dislikes as well as personal preferences in the opposite sex. I have to give a full physical description of myself, as well as a basic medical history complete with questions about how many sexual partners I had in the past. I could have lied. I'm sure people did it all the time, but I was so curious about the damn thing after page after page of questions that I told the truth. I was invested now, I had to make it to the end of the questionnaire and see what this website was all about.

I answered all of the questions. Every damn one and when I finally hit the "submit" button at the bottom of the last page I was directed to *another* page where glowing white text spelled out:

What is your fantasy? What do you desire?

Were they kidding me? This again? I'd written a thousand answers on that damned questionnaire, and now we were finally getting the meat and potatoes, what Little Black Book Club was all about. So I wrote it all out. If they were going to make me waste almost forty-five minutes filling out page after page of personal information, then I was going to lay it all out there and wait for the big nothing. Or maybe it was going to flash to a back page ad, the kind where you pick "dates" out based on pictures and short descriptions. Whatever, it was all a joke anyway.

I want to be pampered, I wrote into the text field. *I want to be completely taken care of from sun up, to sundown. I don't want to have to lift a finger, make a decision, or take care of a single problem. An entire day where someone else is in charge. Just for one day, I don't want to be the boss.*

I hit enter and waited a few seconds. *Stick that in your pipe and smoke it little Black Book Club,* I thought to myself. That was my fantasy, and even I knew it was boring as fuck, but damn it, how nice would it be to let someone else take control for the day. I was tired. I didn't want to do the work anymore. I didn't expect the service to match me up with anything, so I wasn't even remotely disappointed when I was directed to another black screen with little white letters that said, *your profile has been saved. We will contact you when a suitable match has been made.*

Oh for goodness sake, I hadn't expected much, but that had to be one of the biggest letdowns ever after that huge buildup. I must have let Wesley's good looks and exotic smell overwhelm my senses because I don't know why I had even listened to a thing he said.

Little Black Book Club, what a joke.

I was too tired to even be irritated about it for long. The first day of staycation and the most pampering thing I did for myself was put on the cute black silk romper I had stashed in a drawer for paja-mas. It felt cool on my clean and freshly smooth skin, and even though I was just going to sleep at least I could feel pretty in my dreams. My last thought as I snuggled into the bed and pulled the covers up to my chin was, *I'll have to think of at least one interesting thing to do tomorrow, or Blake will make fun of me for wasting my days off.*

FOUR

I DREAMED ABOUT COFFEE. More specifically I dreamed that someone had made the coffee, and that the smell of the glorious liquid permeated the walls of my bedroom and tantalized me with its bitter notes, promising caffeine and warmth in my belly. I also dreamed there was someone else in my apartment with me.

A noise coming from the other room jolted me fully awake and my eyes snapped open.

Shit! Someone was in my apartment!

And they had made coffee?

That didn't make sense, But I definitely smelled the coffee so I peeked my head outside of my bedroom door, and through the open layout of the condo I could see there was indeed someone in my kitchen. A male someone. A *tall* male someone. I could only see his back, with broad shoulders encased in a dark grey dress shirt that tucked into black dress slacks. Black dress slacks that covered what I could already tell was an absolutely phenomenal ass. I hadn't seen someone looking so juicy from the back in...well, I couldn't remember, but this guy looked like he was getting ready to go to work at a high rise downtown, not breaking and entering for breakfast in a strangers apartment.

Noiselessly I crept back into my bedroom and fumbled for my phone to call the police. I wasn't going to be able to sneak out of the condo because I would have to ninja crawl past the Iron Chef in my kitchen, and I knew I couldn't do that, so I needed to call for help. Before I could dial 911 though, I noticed the little green light blinking on my phone that showed I had a message. A voicemail? I didn't recognize the number, and I don't know what part of me decided to throw away my panic and click the button, but I did. I recognized the voice in the recording as soon as he began speaking – Wesley.

"Ms. Beckett, I am pleased that you decided to give our services a try. Your request was met with much enthusiasm, and there were actually several people that wished to be picked to fulfill your needs. Apparently, your request has made you quite popular, Elizabeth. I hope you enjoy your day. From sun up to sun down, I believe you said."

And that was all. There were no instructions, nothing about what to expect or how the strange man had gotten into my house. I had two options. I could either continue my original plan and call the police, or go out into the kitchen and ask some questions. Apparently, The Little Black Book Club had taken me seriously and sent a gigolo out to my house. Now I had to get rid of him.

Taking a deep breath, I turned to leave the bedroom and almost ran smack into the serving tray, being carried by the same man I had only seen from the rear. Looking up I gazed into the most intense blue eyes I had ever seen. Cerulean pools with tinges of brown on the edges, they were amazing. And they were tilted up in the corners with laughter. *The big brute was laughing.*

"You should be in bed," he said as he set the tray down on the nightstand and I was able to see his whole face for the first time. From behind he had looked older, maybe because of the formal clothing. But closer inspection revealed he actually wasn't far from my age, maybe even just a little younger in fact. "I'm glad you didn't call the police on me," he said, a slow grin spreading across his face. He really was quite striking, even if I had to crane my neck to see his face. He had to be six three, six four? I was five foot seven and I only came to his shoulders—he was massive. He could easily overpower me if he wanted to, but instead he brought me a tray. With food on it. And coffee.

"Who are you and what are you doing here?" I'd meant to sound authoritative, but it was difficult to sound in charge when I was wearing my silky pajamas and talking to someone who towered over me.

"I would think you would know that. Didn't you contact the LBBC? Didn't you get a call from Wesley?"

"Well, yes I did but...hey!" I couldn't finish my sentence because he surprised the hell out of me by whisking me straight off my feet and placing me princess style back into the middle of my bed and pulling the covers up over my lap.

"Then there is no misunderstanding. From sun up to sun down, you will let us do all the work. You are not the boss. You are not in charge. My name's

Joshua by the way." He gave me that heart-stopping grin again and I forgot my own name for a minute. He had picked me up like I was nothing and plopped me in bed like a child who had snuck out.

"Yeah, okay full disclosure – I filled out the info form on the website out of curiosity." I twirled my hair in my hands nervously. "I didn't really expect anything from it, and I certainly didn't expect to find a man in my kitchen as soon as I opened my eyeballs this morning. I don't think a voicemail left at eleven thirty at night should be considered sufficient warning. How did you get in here anyway?"

Joshua graced me with another one of those disarming smiles, "I told the girl working the office of your apartment that I was your personal chef and I lost my key. I was supposed to come here and meal prep for the week but I couldn't get in. She didn't give me a hard time about it at all, just went and opened the door for me. I mean, she did ask for identification, but it wasn't that hard. She said you worked a lot, so she wasn't surprised you had someone prepare your meals for you. I think she thought you weren't home or something and I wasn't going to tell her otherwise, I just needed the door open."

I know my mouth was hanging open. I was

sitting in the middle of my bed while a tall, dark and handsome stranger sat on the edge chatting just as casually as you please about how he had conned the office manager into opening my apartment door for him. That wasn't even breaking and entering. That was something else entirely. I didn't know whether to be pissed at the office manager or impressed by Joshua's ingenuity. Maybe it was a little of both.

"You little con artist," I laughed but he didn't, he just cocked his head to the side and looked thoughtful for a moment.

"I think I see what's going on here," he said after a moment of silence. Digging into his pocket he pulled out a slim silver case and took one card from the inside. Here, this what I showed your office manager. It's real, you know, this is what I do for a living."

Joshua Benson – Personal Chef

Heat invaded my face and I knew, just knew, that I was twenty different shades of crimson embarrassment from my obvious faux pax. He was a legitimate personal chef. He was here to cook for me. *From sun up to sun down, I was not to lift a finger.*

Oh my God I practically called him a gigolo.

"I am so sorry," I whimpered as I covered my

hands with my face. "I thought...I thought Little Black Book was an escort service. I'm an idiot."

His response was laughter, loud and long. He didn't look angry, but he was vastly amused. It was the misunderstanding of a lifetime, but he seemed to be taking it well—me assuming he was a prostitute.

"Ms. Beckett," he began, but I cut him off with a wave of my hand.

"I would think at this point in our incredibly weird relationship you can call me Elizabeth." I was dying of embarrassment and him using formal speech with me was just making it worse.

"Elizabeth," he began again. "Did you think I was coming here to have sex with you?"

My hands covered my face again and I knew I was acting like a child, but I couldn't help it. I couldn't even look him in the eyes at this point. "I'm sorry. I thought you were an escort service."

He didn't get angry like I thought he might. Instead he sighed, "Yeah, I can see how we could be misrepresented that way. Especially because Wesley keeps such an air of mysteriousness about the company. But the truth is, Little Black Book Club does provide a service of fulfilling fantasies. Although I did read your profile—it didn't say anything about sex." Joshua's blue eyes darkened and he leaned in closer, "Although if that's what you want I'm not opposed."

His face was inches from mine, his eyes impossibly blue and staring straight into my soul. I was frozen, but he made no other movements towards me. He was simply waiting for me to say something.

"You're teasing me," I said when I found my breath and my scattered thoughts. I was rewarded with another panty-melting smile.

"Maybe," he said, eyes sparkling as he stood up and straightened the covers around me. "Maybe not. I will tell you this, I am here to cook for you. All three meals and anything you should want in between." He grabbed the tray that he had set down previously and placed it gently into my lap. Next to a cup of coffee was a covered plate like we used in the hotel to keep food warm as it was being delivered by room service. As he removed the lid and set it down on the nightstand I was treated to a most surprising sight. Crepes. Three strawberry crepes nestled against each other in the middle of the plate while plump glazed strawberries glistened against the pale pastry. My stomach grumbled loudly.

"Your coffee is getting cold," Joshua said disapprovingly, "I'll get you another cup." As he leaned down to pick the cup up off the tray he gently moved the hair off my shoulder and away from my ear. I hadn't been expecting it, I mean, I hadn't expected a single thing that had happened so far this morning but I was really surprised when he whispered in my ear.

"I know you said you didn't want sex," I shuddered at his closeness and the sensation of his breath on my skin. "But Nicholas is going to be here soon. He's going to take one look at you and forget what he is supposed to be doing here. If I were you, and you don't want to encourage him, I would change out of that sexy as fuck lingerie you are wearing and put on something that makes you look a little less appealing. Like, I don't know, some body armor or something." Joshua paused to blow gently on the skin of my neck. "Unless you changed your mind and you *do* want sex, then all you have to do is say the word and Nicholas will have you on your back and screaming his name in a matter of minutes. He'll make you think it was your idea too. I'll help."

Joshua hadn't even touched me, but my mind had already gone to an incredibly wild place, and even though I hadn't moved at all, his words had brought my body to a fever pitch. Who was Nicholas, and why was I already thinking about him in such a way? Joshua pulled away and took my coffee cup with him. "I'll be in the kitchen cleaning up, eat your breakfast Elizabeth." And then he was gone, leaving me aching in several places and staring stupidly down at the tray in my lap.

FIVE

BREAKFAST WAS DIVINE. I had zero complaints about any of it, except for the awkward blush staining my cheeks after Joshua's whispered confession. Never mind the way my thighs had clenched tightly together when he had mentioned the name Nicholas. I'd already misinterpreted what Joshua was supposed to be doing, what was this Nicholas' job supposed to be? Liquid heat pooled between my legs as I thought about Joshua's words. He'd been teasing me, hadn't he? I should have been aggravated by the intrusion, by the miscommunication, by the blatant liberties a strange man was taking in my home.

Instead, it was exhilarating.

I had no plans on sleeping with a stranger, not that I had any kind of personal hang-up about one night stands. People do all kinds of things in the name of a good time. Sharing your body with another consenting adult is probably low on the list of terrible ways to spend a few hours. But just because I don't have the time to meet men and form personal connections doesn't mean I don't want to. I was lonely just like everyone else was. I didn't plan on sleeping with the handsome chef in the kitchen, but if he was going to continue to tease me with the promise of a good time, then I just might change my mind.

At least that was what I thought to myself as I took extra care in the shower. Washing my hair and shaving even though I had just done it the day before. As I soaped up my skin and slid my hands up and down my body, I imagined it was Joshua's hands, not mine, working the lather over my skin. Lingering in the soft places until my breasts tingled and my breath came in quick gasps. I couldn't even be the least bit embarrassed that I was touching myself in the shower, thinking about the possibility of not just one, but two strangers having their wicked way with me. It wasn't what I had been thinking about when I signed up on the Little Black Book website, but holy shit was I thinking about it now. How could I not when he had said such a suggestive thing to me?

I couldn't think of anything else.

The shower was a little longer than it should have been, mostly because I was so worked up thinking of the young chef's hands on my body that I couldn't stop touching myself long enough to finish washing. I couldn't bring myself to satisfaction though, not with Joshua in the next room and only a couple of thin walls between us. I was pretty worked up, but it seemed like not even my imagination was good enough to get a quick O before I met my next guest.

When had I become so repressed?

The next guest had already arrived by the time I got out of the shower. I heard the voices in the kitchen and before I could tell myself it was a bad idea I threw on a robe and peeked around the corner to get a look. They were standing almost shoulder to shoulder in front of the sink with their backs to me. Joshua was cutting vegetables, I assumed prepping for lunch, and the newcomer was standing next to him watching. From the back I could see he had longer chestnut colored hair that fell in light waves to just brush his collar. He wore a pair of dark denim pants – casual, with a light blue polo tucked in at the waist. He was probably average height but standing next to someone as tall as Joshua he just seemed so much slighter in stature. They were murmuring low to each other, but I could still pick out the words.

"So tell me what she's like, Josh," the newcomer stated, and I was surprised at the depth of his tone. I had just assumed that he was younger because of his stature, but his voice was that of a mature man in his prime.

"She's just as hot as Wesley said she was," Joshua said as he continued to cut a cucumber in short even strokes, placing the slices in a small bowl on the counter. My cheeks warmed at the compliment, both because Joshua thought I was good looking and because Wesley said so too.

"Nice," the stranger said as he swiped a cucumber from the cutting board before Joshua had a chance to nab it. He popped it into his mouth and chewed. "This should be fun," he said once he'd swallowed his bite. He shoulder bumped Joshua playfully, and it was clear that these two men knew each other, but Joshua shook his head sadly.

"She's not into it."

"What do you mean she's not into it?" The wavy-haired man sounded confused.

"Wesley said we weren't allowed to do anything she didn't want to do, and she pretty much told me no sex not more than twenty minutes ago before she got in the shower." Joshua sounded put out, like he had been looking forward to something I didn't even know was on the table.

"So what, you are just going to cook today?" The other man asked the question like he couldn't believe that was all that was going on.

"Yep," Joshua said, sounding utterly disappointed, sliding the rest of the cucumber slices into the bowl and reaching for a bright round tomato. "And it looks like you are here for a regular old afternoon massage. A professional one, Nicholas." He emphasized the last part as he started slicing into the tomato.

So this was Nicholas.

Another little thrill ran through me as I thought about what Joshua had said about Nicholas earlier. About what he would do to me if I let him. My breasts tingled, and my nipples tightened into hard points as I drew my robe even tighter together in the front. I was peeping. In my own house even. But damn if I couldn't look away yet. I wanted to know what else they were going to say, what other secrets they would divulge.

Nicholas turned then, but he didn't look in my direction. I was still concealed in my hiding place where I stood slightly behind the wall, barely able to see around the corner. I caught sight of his profile and he looked quite young. Younger than Joshua and I anyway. He just had such a deep timbre in his voice that he seemed so much older.

"Well, that's okay I guess if that's what she wants," Nicholas said as he reached one hand and patted Joshua on the back. "What about you? Are you going to be okay?"

Why would he ask that?

"I'll be fine," Joshua replied, and I might have been mistaken but he sounded a little sad. "I'm here to give her what she needs, and if all she needs is food from me then that is what she'll get. She won't lift a finger, from sun up to sun down." He repeated the same words from earlier and hearing them repeated out loud so many times was just plain embarrassing.

"She's way too high strung and overworked." Joshua continued. "She needs to relax. She needs you and your magic hands."

Nicholas ceased with his casual patting and let his arm slide down Joshua's back in a strangely intimate gesture. "But what about your needs?" Nicholas asked, concern lacing his voice. "Who's taking care of you?" And the other arm, the one not lingering on Joshua's back, crept around the front of his body. My mouth dropped open in shock as I heard the metallic slip of a zipper sliding down and saw Joshua stiffen, a slight tremble in his hands that still clutched the knife he had been cutting tomatoes with.

He did turn then, just to face Nicholas, not enough to see me in my hiding place, just enough to reveal what was going on. Nicholas had his hand down the front of Joshua's open pants and was rubbing circles with his thumb over the cloth covering Joshua's cock.

And from the way he had his eyes closed and his head thrown back, Joshua loved it.

Shit, that was hot.

Never mind the fact that both of these men were complete strangers, or that I had no idea what was going to happen in the next five minutes much less the rest of the entire day, but I had never seen a man touch another man like that. It was fascinating. I leaned forward to get a better look and noticed the lump in the front of Joshua's pants growing larger as Nicholas pressed and massaged his way through the opening in his slacks.

"Joshua, look at you." Nicholas chided in a low voice as he kept up his ministrations, kneading harder, sliding his hand even deeper down the front of Joshua's pants. "You aren't taking care of yourself like you should." Then the hand that had been on Joshua's back slipped around to the front, and now both of Nicholas's hands were rubbing Joshua down.

He couldn't hold on to the knife any longer and let it clatter to the cutting board as he leaned over and braced himself on the counter with both hands.

"You...have to stop." He panted, although his words expressed the opposite. Even though his voice pleaded with Nicholas to cease, Joshua still moaned low in his throat and pressed his hips forward, trying to get closer to those busy hands.

"Stop what?" Nicholas asked, teeth biting down on his lower lip as one busy hand slid around to grab Joshua's ass, pushing his pants further down in the process. "Didn't you say I had magic hands?" Desire shot through my body as he leaned forward and licked Joshua's neck before biting the skin there. Sucking it into his mouth while simultaneously working his cock and ass through the fabric of his pants.

"Fuck, Nick. I said that because you are a fucking masseuse and your job is to give Elizabeth a massage, not stroke me off in the kitchen." But the words were lost as he pinned Nicholas to the counter and devoured his open mouth, the hands that had been bracing him against the counter now trapping Nicholas in place. Not like he wanted to escape. Nicholas had baited Joshua, and now that his self-control had snapped he was relishing in the punishment. Clearly, these two men already had a history. A sexual history.

How taboo.

I moved farther into the kitchen without conscious thought, away from my hiding place around the corner. My thighs damp with arousal, I had never seen anything so erotic in my life as these two men with their hands all over each other. I needed to see more, I wanted to see how far they would go. It didn't matter that this was a massive setup, a play put on for me in response to my curious inquiry. Each stroke of their hands on each other's flesh felt like a stroke against my own and I felt feverish...hot. This was definitely a fantasy. One I never even known that I had.

Nicholas broke free of the kiss and pulled his hands out of Joshua's pants, placing both palms against his chest, grabbing at the fabric of his shirt and pulling him close. "Cut the shit Josh, I know what you like and I know what you want. You want me to free that thick cock of yours and hit my knees right now don't you?" Joshua closed his eyes and shook his head no, obviously fighting against the desire that Nicholas's words brought out in him.

"Yes, you do." Nicholas was already sinking to his knees on the grey and white tile, hands moving back down to Joshua's pants and reaching into the waistband of his black boxer briefs. Joshua still had his eyes closed, but his hips twitched in response. Mine did too if I was honest. I don't think I had ever wanted anything as bad in my life as I wanted to watch Nicholas wrap his lips around Joshua's cock. My own mouth watered at the thought.

Joshua kept his eye closed but moaned again, and Nicholas must have taken it as some sort of permission because he pulled the pants completely down, taking the black boxer briefs with them, revealing Joshua all the way. Long, hard and completely smooth, his cock pointed straight out, throbbing, reaching for the promise of Nicholas's mouth. Joshua might have been trying to resist, but his dick definitely had other ideas.

And I wanted to see it all.

"Elizabeth will see," Joshua ground out as he fisted his hands in the chestnut colored hair. To pull him closer or to push him away, I didn't know. He seemed to be fighting his own demons, but his body was winning over his mind.

Nicholas leaned in and placed a wet open-mouthed kiss on the inside of Joshua's thigh before he turned and looked me right in the eyes. There was no surprise on his face at all as his lips curved into a wicked grin. "Hell yes she will. She's been here watching the entire time. Open your eyes man, and look—look at her face. She wants me to suck you off too. Ask her. Hello, Elizabeth," he said as he stroked his hand up and down Joshua's length, completely unconcerned that I had been peeping on them for the last ten minutes or so. "I'm Nicholas, nice to meet you."

Joshua's eyes snapped open, blazing deep blue and clouded with need. I couldn't even be embarrassed at what was happening in my kitchen because nobody else was. Neither of the men was surprised to see me standing there, completely naked under my robe, almost panting with my need to see them touch each other more. A thought slipped into my mind, cutting through the haze of desire that had descended over me. They both knew I was there the whole time. They weren't embarrassed at being caught, no *they wanted to be caught*.

Nicholas never stopped stroking his hands up and down Joshua's length, and he thrust into the touch, becoming even longer and thicker, if that was even possible. Both men looked at me expectantly, waiting for me to say something, not willing to continue without permission but not wanting to be stopped either. I opened my mouth to speak, my words were either going to fuel the fire and lead them to orgasm or splash water on the entire thing and quite possibly end my day of fantasy.

"You want me to watch you, don't you Joshua? You both do."

SIX

HE DIDN'T EVEN HAVE the nerve to look embarrassed, just smiled another one of those slow smiles he had gifted me with earlier while his gaze raked over my body. I was acutely aware in that moment that I was standing a few feet away from them in nothing but a half tied robe, with my nipples drawn up so painfully hard that surely they must be visible through the thin silk. Nicholas kept pumping Joshua slowly, lazily, watching me through hooded eyes, waiting for me to give approval. They both needed the words.

"I love to be watched," Joshua said and licked his lips. My eyes followed the path of his tongue, and I wondered what it would feel like tracing along my skin. Hadn't I just said earlier that I wasn't even thinking about sex? Suddenly I couldn't think about anything else.

"You told me there wouldn't be any sex," Joshua continued, and he looked disappointed when he said it, but then grunted in pleasure as Nicholas chose that moment to cup his balls with the hand he wasn't using to jack him off. "And if you continue to say it, then I won't pressure you. But there are so many ways to pleasure each other Elizabeth, and I think the thought of Nicholas touching me makes you wet. I bet your pussy just throbs thinking of him sliding my cock in his mouth doesn't it?"

Fuck yes it does.

I couldn't even speak, the words got caught in a strangled moan. So turned on I couldn't even give them the words they wanted, I could only nod my head in approval. *Yes. Please. Do this thing. Let me watch you pleasure each other.* Blood roared in my ears and it took all my self-control not to beg them to touch me too. I was witnessing something I had never thought I would ever see. This was a treat for my eyes, I would be a fool to put a stop to it.

"Come here Elizabeth," Joshua commanded. I had previously thought that Nicholas had been the domi-nant one, but now, with Joshua's gaze boring into me, commanding me to obey, I wondered why I had ever thought he wasn't in control. He wanted me to come, so I went. I stood next to the two of them, not sure what I should do or say, until Joshua slipped one hand into the front of my robe and stroked his thumb across one tight nipple and I shivered, dropping the edges of the navy silk that I had been clutching together. The es of my robe fell open and Joshua took advantage, grabbing me by the tits and squeezing roughly. *God, it hurt so good*.

"So sensitive, Elizabeth. That's good, I don't know why you would want to deny yourself that feeling. Keep your eyes on us," he said as he unbuttoned his shirt and let it fall to the floor. Nicholas let go of him long enough for Joshua to step out of his pants and stand completely nude before us. He was mouth-wateringly perfect. Smooth, tanned skin stretched tight over lean muscle. His firm round ass flexing as Nicholas caught him with his hands again. Pulling and kneading with a little more energy, clearly impatient to get moving. For a moment I was jealous, wishing it was me on my knees in front of Joshua, longing to take him into my mouth, sliding my tongue along the sensitive skin and feeling him twitch in response. I reached my hand out before I could think better of it but Joshua caught my hands before I could touch him.

"No touching yet, Elizabeth." He chuckled warmly, bringing my hands to his mouth and kissing the knuckles gently. "Watch us for now. And when you watch Nicholas make me come, and he is finished swallowing every drop I give him, then I'll ask you the question again. If you want me to touch you, then you can tell me. But right now, be patient, and tell Nicholas what you want him to do. What we both want him to do."

A thousand dirty thoughts raced through my mind at Joshua's decree. I wasn't myself anymore. I was someone else. Some other woman with no inhibitions who wanted nothing more than to watch one man bring another to orgasm in front of me. It sounded a hundred miles away as I heard myself say, in a voice bolder than I had ever used before, "Put his cock in your mouth Nicholas. Show me how bad you want to suck his dick."

And oh, but he did.

Nicholas wasted no time sliding his lips onto Joshua's rigid length, bobbing on the head and gripping gently at the base with both hands. Joshua closed his eyes again, fisting his hands in Nicholas's hair, guiding him as he lifted his head up and down. "Fuck yes, Nick, more. You can take more of me I know it. Don't act like a virgin for Elizabeth's sake, show her what you can do. Fucking take all of me, choke on my cock."

His filthy words had me drenched, my own wetness slipping down my thighs, but it was nothing compared to what they did for Nicholas. Joshua's words spurred him on, and he took all of that length into his mouth, deep throating until his cheeks puffed out and saliva slipped out of his mouth and pooled around the base of Joshua's dick. Desire burned away all doubts, all inhibitions that had been lingering inside of me. I wanted to touch. *I had to touch.*

Having completely lost control of my own body I reached out and cupped his balls in my hand, rolling them gently while Nicholas continued to gobble on his cock like he was starving. "Oh God, yes Elizabeth." Joshua groaned, and as I slipped my hand from his balls to lightly grasp the base of his dick and gently twist, he took one of his hands from Nicholas's hair and wrapped it around mine. Squeezing his hand over mine until I was gripping him tightly, a cock ring of flesh, Joshua thrust himself between my fingers. The action forced him even deeper into Nicholas' mouth, making both Nicholas and I moan in tandem. I could come like this, without being touched, feeling the pleasure these men were giving each other. I kept one hand on Joshua and the other I ran through Nicholas's hair, giving it a tug, pulling his head down even further. He responded with another moan that traveled through Joshua to me, I felt it on the hand that I kept wrapped around Joshua's hard length.

Watching Joshua slide in and out of Nicholas's mouth, made me feel as if he was pushing in and out of me as well, and my legs trembled. Being connected to this erotic act was too much for them to keep me standing. I sank to my knees beside Nicholas, my hand still in his hair, his mouth bumping against my fingers as he continued to deep throat Joshua. I felt like I was being fucked on my kitchen floor instead of being a spectator. I didn't know how I would feel later, but as of this moment, I was grateful that I had been curious enough to follow the instructions on the card for the Little Black Book Club.

I felt the tremors run through his body before Joshua even spoke.

"Nick, I'm going to come—swallow it all." He commanded. I didn't know who had the position of more power, Joshua, standing taller than anyone else and giving orders, or Nicholas on his knees, controlling every bit of pleasure Joshua felt. I was fascinated by it all. I gripped Joshua tightly as he came, feeling the pumps and twitches as Nicholas's mouth filled and he did exactly as he was told, swallowing every drop, letting nothing escape. And when he was finished, and Joshua slid out of his mouth for the last time, Nicholas turned to me, the pupils of his eyes blown wide with lust.

"Well Elizabeth," Nicholas said, still on his knees next to me. "How was it? Did you enjoy watching?" I looked up at Joshua from my place on the floor, my hands slipping over the silk covering my breasts, feeling the nipples pebble up under the fabric. The pressure building up inside of me was so intense, I had to do something to release it, so I pinched my nipples hard between my fingers and gasped at the pleasure and the pain of it. I needed more. I needed to be touched, but I also wanted to see...more.

Joshua stood over us both, his breath coming in short gasps but he was still in a position of authority, at least over Nicholas and me as we stayed kneeling on the floor. I was practically begging for release. "You need help Elizabeth. No lifting a finger remember? You shouldn't have to please yourself when we are right here. We're here for you, remember?"

That was easy for him to say when he was the only one out of the three of us who had just had an orgasm, but I would be lying if I said I didn't enjoy watching them. I fucking loved it. Was I becoming a sexual deviant?

"Elizabeth," Joshua said, still standing naked and proud before me. "What will it be? Do you want me to put my clothes back on and finish prepping lunch? Nicholas brought his massage table and he really is a very talented professional." The talented professional was currently getting to his feet and sporting a raging boner. But I had eaten Joshua's crepes for breakfast, and knowing how good he was at his actual job I had no doubt Nicholas was as well. I had no doubt that lunch would be fabulous, and a massage from Nicholas would be incredible, but I had just opened a door inside of myself that I hadn't even known was there. A sinful door. A sexual awakening that was brought about by two men pleasuring each other in my kitchen while I watched, not a part of it yet not separate either. There was more I wanted to explore.

Looking up at Joshua I chose my words carefully. Whatever I said next would direct the flow of activities for the rest of the day and I would be damned if I would waste a single second pretending I didn't want what I wanted. Real like would be waiting two days from now, and I would have to go back to my boring life of service to others. Right now though, I was at the mercy of the two virile young strangers plucking at dark parts of me that I hadn't even known existed. So I sucked in a deep breath, worried my lower lip with my teeth and said the only thing I could, the truth of what was on my mind.

"What else will you let me watch you do?"

SEVEN

BOTH MEN STARED at me with surprise stamped across their faces. "What?" I asked when their eyebrows disappeared into their hairlines. "You asked. That was hot. I've never seen anything so hot in my entire life and I know you enjoyed putting on that show for me. You wanted to know how I felt so I'm telling you. I want to see more."

"Don't you want me to make you feel good?" Completely comfortable in his nakedness, Joshua stared down at me, incredulous. "Don't get me wrong, I love messing around with Nick but to be honest, I was kind of hoping you would come out of your shell a bit. And seeing you still kneeling on the floor like that makes me want to...mess you up.

I couldn't say anything for a moment, just knelt on the floor with my robe hanging wide open, trapped in the deep ocean blue of his eyes. I didn't know what "mess you up" meant, but it sounded dirty, and my body reacted. *Yes, please. I want that too.* My lips parted, and I ran my tongue over them nervously. Joshua's eyes narrowed, and he took a step forward, reaching down to help me up. I was certain he wanted to do more than that, but as I rose to my feet and Joshua's head bent to capture my lips with his, I heard discreet coughing. I ran my tongue around the outside of his mouth before turning my head to acknowledge Nicholas.

"Jealous?" I asked, grasping at a boldness I didn't know I possessed. This was my first time looking at Nicholas, really looking his full face and not just a side profile, and my goodness he was stunning. Light brown eyes that slanted upward on the corners, a slim nose and wide mouth. His hair had been messed up by both mine and Joshua's hands and was currently spread around his face like a lion's mane. He looked feral...hungry. Sexual intent radiated from him as he leaned towards us, intensity blazing from his gold-tinged eyes.

"Jealous?" He whispered when he was as close to Joshua and me as he could be without touching us. So close I could feel the energy buzzing from his skin. "Jealously would imply that you are offering something to Josh that I can't have." Joshua slipped my useless robe from around my shoulders, letting it puddle at my feet as he dropped light kisses across my collarbone, leaving a damp trail that made me shiver when the cool air hit my skin. I wanted to close my eyes and give myself up to the sensation of Joshua's mouth on my skin, but I couldn't look away from Nicholas's fierce gaze.

Had I thought the air was cool? Staring back at Nicholas my skin was ablaze with heat. And need. He was teasing me, I was hiding nothing from him but offering myself fully. To both of them.

"Are you, Elizabeth?" Nicholas said as he lightly traced over my bare breasts with one blunt tipped finger. "Offering something to Joshua that I can't have?" The moan was ripped from my throat as Joshua tipped my head back and licked the side of my neck before biting down. Not too hard, but hard enough to send electricity screaming through my fingertips. My toes. My breasts. The juncture at my thighs.

I was lost.

Eyes closed, head rolling back while Joshua licked and sucked at the skin of my neck I reached for Nicholas. He was still fully clothed, more's the pity, and I grabbed the fabric of his polo shirt and pulled him close. Closer still, until the full front of him was pressed against the front of me and I could feel the hardness of his raging erection pressed against me in the most delicious spot. His mouth came crashing down on mine. Hot. Wet. Claiming.

Punishing.

He was feeling left out, and how dare I forget that he too, was here to give me pleasure? To take care of me for the day? I wouldn't choose between the two of them, I would take from them both, whatever they could give me. Then I would feed on the memories after they left and I returned to my normal life. I wouldn't be the same though. I knew it. This was life altering, this was carnal, this was a change in the chemical properties of my mind. Pushing past sexual boundaries and welcoming the different. The new.

I wanted them both and I wanted them now. Even if they weren't really mine, just for today I could pretend.

Leaning backward into Joshua, I wrapped both arms around Nicholas's neck, letting the waves of his hair cascade over them. I tasted the remnants of Joshua on his lips, the memory of what he had just been doing sending liquid heat spreading through my limbs. Whimpering, I pulled him closer, closer still until there wasn't room for even air between our bodies. Two sets of hands reached under me, and two sets of arms lifted me up until my bottom was perched on the countertop. Free from having to hold myself up I wrapped both legs around Nicholas's waist and hooked my ankles across his back, pressing myself firmly against his hardness. He moaned into my open mouth, the denim of his jeans scraping roughly against my thighs. I didn't care. For the first time in probably my entire life I was turned the fuck on, and the only way to flip the switch would be to give me what I wanted, what I craved.

Growling, Nicholas broke our kiss. "Fuck the rules, Josh, I'm taking her." *Oh, that sounded so animalistic*, and my thighs twitched at the thought. *Wait a minute...rules?*

"Whoa, Nick, we promised." Joshua lifted his head from my shoulder and his hands stilled on my breasts. "We can do a lot of things, but we can't do that."

"Says who?" I said, disbelief in my tone. I didn't know exactly what they were talking about, but they had me roused to a fever pitch and now I felt as if cold water had been splashed down on me." And what exactly, can you not do?"

Joshua didn't answer right away, just stood there

with his hand on Nicholas's shoulder while Nicholas still stared at me with his intense golden gaze. He was still an exotic beast, and he was looking at me like I was prey. *God, I want to be prey.*

"You know what we agreed to," Joshua said softly fingers digging into Nicholas's shoulder. "You know what *he* wants."

"Right now, *I* want." Nicholas spoke the words while grinding his teeth in irritation. He finally turned to look at Joshua, and there was something in his gaze that took some of the strain from his shoulders. Nicholas's hands fell away from me and he took a step back.

"What about what *I* want," I asked the room. "Is that not why you two are here in the first place? I mean you've worked pretty hard to get me to come around to the idea of sex with you, and now that I'm saying yes please—let's fucking do this thing—you are telling me *no*?" I hopped down from the counter and grabbed my robe from the where it had puddled on the floor, a cold pool of navy blue silk. Wrapping it around my shoulders and belting it around my waist angrily I muttered, "What in the hell kind of game is this? How humiliating...."

I had every intention of stalking from the room and going to my bedroom to get dressed. My flame had been doused, my ardor cooled at the embarrassment of being brought to the peak of wanting and then left to flounder. Humiliating wasn't even a strong enough word. Hurt maybe? Yeah, that was more like it. I didn't make it far, not even back to the hallway where I had been hiding previously before I was spun around and pinned to the wall.

A flurry of chestnut hair passed in front of my eyes and then I was nose to nose with Nicholas, who took my hand and pressed it firmly against the front of his jeans. "Do not doubt," he said, his voice so low it was more like a rumble than anything else, "that *this* is for you." And then he kissed me again, softly, gently, like he wasn't pressing me against the wall and my fingers weren't surrounding his bulge.

"I don't know what's happening to me," I whispered as he broke the kiss, letting my bottom lip slide slowly out of his mouth. He looked irritated. "What is your agreement? With whom? Is it Wesley?"

Joshua barked a short laugh from farther in the kitchen. He had pulled his pants back on but remained shirtless and had picked up the chef's knife again and was calmly slicing tomatoes like didn't just have his dick sucked in the kitchen mere moments ago.

"Josh, did you wash your hands?"

Joshua had the grace to look wounded. "Nick, I'm a professional. Of course I washed my hands. Now stop being cryptic and tell her what's going on. I don't want to ruin this day with secrets. I still have plans for her." He paused his slicing to pin me with another one of his laser-like stares, "I don't need to put my dick in you to make you orgasm, Elizabeth. Test me." And then he finished slicing the tomato and slid it into a waiting bowl.

Jesus.

"OK, so Elizabeth we sort of have a gentleman's agreement with someone else. Not Wesley." Nicholas emphasized the last part. "Our agreement with Wesley is that we take care of *you*, in the way that you need taken care of. He doesn't place those kinds of restrictions on us because the restrictions are placed on us by you, Elizabeth."

"The client, you mean?" It was a snotty remark but I was still feeling kind of snappy.

"We're all clients, Elizabeth," Joshua said from his position at the counter. "That's how Little Black Book Club works. It's not an escort service, it's more of a fantasy matchmaking service. People are matched up based on their desires and needs."

"You desire a break in your routine, the

monotony of always having to be in charge. Of always having to be in *control*." Nicholas was right on that point.

"So you guys aren't employees then?" I asked Nicholas, but it was Joshua who answered.

"Oh no, Wesley doesn't need employees. He's a master at examining a client and making excellent matches. I'm matched with you because he wanted someone who would be gentle and take care of you. I'm very non-threatening, aren't I?" And he threw me a wink. He was right. He'd managed to weasel right into my condo even going so far as to get a key from the office manager. He'd wiggled right into my good graces immediately. I had never felt threatened by Joshua in the least. Raging lust, yes. Threatened, no.

"Then what is your fantasy, Joshua?" I asked carefully, although I might have already known the answer. "What is it that you desire?"

"Besides smoking hot brunettes with big tits they keep hidden behind blue bathrobes?" This time it was Nicholas teasing me, and I started to relax again. I couldn't help it, his smile was disarming when he didn't look like he wanted to fuck me brainless.

Joshua smiled at Nicholas's antics. "Besides that? Well, I like to be watched. There's something exciting about not knowing how the person looking on is going to react. Will they be disgusted? Will they be embarrassed? Will they be turned on?" Joshua flashed another one of those panty incinerating smiles, the kind that promised he could get me out of that robe again without me even knowing how it happened. "I knew you were there from the minute I heard the water shut off in the shower. I heard your footsteps down the hall. I smelled your strawberry kiwi shampoo. I was hard as stone thinking about Nicholas touching me in front of you, and you hiding in the shadows enjoying the whole thing. I'm getting hard again just thinking about it, fuck."

I had to tear my eyes away then, away from Joshua standing at my kitchen counter wearing nothing but those dark slacks, the muscles of his abdomen flexing above the waistband as he talked about how hot it made him that I had watched him get groped. They weren't doing a very good job of calming me down, that was for sure.

"And what about you?" I asked Nicholas, who was still standing entirely too close for me to get a full breath of air. His eyes still too intense to be just friendly, the bulge in his pants letting me know just how hot he still was and that he had a tendency to hang to the left.

"What about me?" He breathed, and the puff of

air blew against my cheek. If he wanted me to lose my libido, he would need to give me some more space.

"What's your fantasy? Why are you here?"

"Right now my fantasy is you, losing that robe and letting me do dirty things to you." I shivered at his words and fresh desire pooled between my legs. "But I came today because I like Josh's dick." He smiled, a hint of real humor in his eyes. "I'd be a happy man if you would tell me I get both today."

Jesus, how was I going to survive these two?

"How about we take a break?" I squeaked as I slipped past Nicholas and went over to see what Joshua was putting together. "I saw we eat whatever delicious food Joshua is making, and you both tell me about whoever *he* is, that you have an agreement with, and what it has to do with me, okay?"

"Fine," Nicholas said, coming up behind me and swiping a pinch of parmesan cheese off the plate Joshua had been grating over. "But after lunch you let me get you on my table and put my *magic hands* on you." He must have seen the question in my eyes because he continued, "I brought my massage table. It's my job. It's what I was sent here to do."

"You'll end up falling asleep." Joshua murmured as he stole the plate of cheese away from Nicholas and went back to fixing lunch, some sort of pasta dish and a garden salad from what I could tell.

"She will not," Nicholas countered, looking offended.

"She might. He's really very good at massage. You may get so relaxed you fall asleep."

"Well, if that's what happens when she's relaxed then that's what happens. Don't worry Elizabeth. I'll take care of you."

I bet you will, I said. But only in my head. It wouldn't be good to encourage him after we had just gotten settled down.

EIGHT

LUNCH WAS AMAZING. Pasta mama with sunny eggs and parmesan cheese complimented by a fresh garden salad and mimosas. It was an easy meal, shared with the two men I felt strangely comfortable around after the ménage that almost happened on my kitchen floor. My belly was full and my skin was flushed with the champagne, but I still didn't have my answers.

"So who's *he*?" I asked when the dishes had been cleared, and Nicholas began working on setting up the massage table in the front room. My apartment had an open floor plan, so I had a clear view of him from my spot at the kitchen table. "What does he have to do with me, and does he have a name?"

"Yeah, he has a name," Nicholas called over his shoulder as he set up some bottles of what I assumed were massage lotions on the end table in the front room. "But we aren't allowed to say it." He pulled a thick fluffy towel from the bag that he had brought with him and laid it across the massage table. It was a professional set up all right, Nicholas knew what he was doing.

"What do you mean you aren't allowed to say it?"

"He means you aren't allowed to know it." Joshua moved around the kitchen, cleaning up after lunch and pulling more food out of the refrigerator, prepping for dinner, I assumed. "Part of your issue is wanting to not be in charge for once. Well, this guy is definitely used to being in charge. Apparently not knowing his name just adds to the mystery."

"I don't know how comfortable I am with that." And I didn't. That sounded scary.

"Relax Elizabeth, we wouldn't let anything bad happen to you." This was from Nicholas, who had finished setting up and was waiting patiently for me to join him in the other room. "And I don't get a bad vibe from this guy. I think he knows just what you need, more so than we do, and I think it will be good for you. Besides, no one is going to do anything you don't want. That's the hard and firm rule we all abide by."

Hard and firm. Did he really just say that?

By the grin that stretched across his face I knew he meant the double entendre. Silly Nicholas. I would be sad when he had to leave. When they both had to leave, and I would have to go back to my normal life and pretend that I had never met them. But that was hours from now. I still had plenty of hours of sunlight left to enjoy their company.

"Wesley wouldn't match you with someone he didn't trust to have your best interests in mind," Joshua said the words firmly. I could tell by his tone that he meant every one of them. I envied their absolute trust in the older man. I didn't have that kind of trust in anyone, and that was probably the biggest part of my problem. I didn't trust anyone enough and that was why I always had to be in control in my professional as well as my personal life. I could never let go and trust that someone else could handle things. Well, Wesley had done a bang up job so far, maybe I could trust him in this too.

"Are you coming in here or what?" Nicholas gestured impatiently, standing next to his table with his eyebrows raised. I laughed and wandered into the front room.

"Thank you for the amazing lunch Joshua," I called back into the kitchen. "I'm getting ready for my nap now." Joshua grinned and gave me a two-fingered salute before he went back to whatever he was working on. It would be delicious, whatever it was I was certain.

"I don't know where you pulled this sass from," Nicholas said as he patted the table next to him, "but I like it. Now ditch the robe and get on the table. Belly down. Don't worry," he said when I raised my eyebrows in question, "I have a sheet to protect your modesty, my lady."

Never one to back down from a challenge, I dropped the robe and let it puddle at my feet for the second time that day. Taking my sweet time getting on to the table I let Nicholas's eyes feast on my naked body, watching his gaze turn from light brown to gold again. He knew I was playing with him, but he let me. He deserved it. True to his word, once I was lying on the table he covered me from the waist down with the sheet. Sweeping my hair to the side and over one shoulder he asked, so close to me that his breath caressed my bare shoulder, "Any allergies I should know about before I pick an oil?"

"None that I know of," I murmured, already starting to relax before his hands even touched me. He had a heated pad on the table, below the fluffy towel, and the warmth seeped into my bones, luring me to close my eyes. God, his hands felt good.

kneading my tense muscles, working away the heavy stresses that had worn me down for so long. Joshua was right, Nicholas had magic hands. I don't know how long I laid like that, in a twilight consciousness, but it was Joshua's voice that broke the spell and brought me back.

"Told you she would fall asleep."

I moved my head slightly until I was looking to the side, my cheek pressed into the soft padding of the table. "I'm not sleeping." I didn't think I was anyway, but I certainly didn't notice when Joshua came into the room and sat down on the couch either. He still didn't have a shirt on, just lounging on my couch like he owned it, his tanned skin a stark contrast to the pale cream of my sofa. He caught me staring and grinned. I smiled back.

"Elizabeth can do what she wants to do when I have my hands on her," Nicholas said cheekily, as his hands worked the muscles in my lower back. His palms crept down to the soft globes of my ass, pressing, fingers seeking. I moaned low in my throat. I hadn't meant to, but his hands were doing things to my lower body. I know he wasn't doing it on purpose, that he was giving me a legitimately professional massage, but I couldn't help it. I was thinking about earlier when he'd been on his knees on my kitchen floor, and I was instantly wet again.

"Elizabeth you can't make those noises and expect me to behave myself." Nicholas, the voice of reason, admonished me. His words made sense, but his hands stopped their professional ministrations and began a soothing, circular rubbing, his thumbs pressing into my cheeks, spreading them apart gently prodding closer to that throbbing part of me I dimly realized that at some point he had ditched the sheet covering me and it was just his hands on my bare skin. The massage oil allowing his fingertips and palms to glide over me, warming me.

It was too good.

"I can't help it," I mewled into to table cushion. "Your hands are so close. Please Nicholas, I ache." I was talking to Nicholas, but I was looking at Joshua. He was the one I needed to convince. He was the one who would try to stop us with his logic and reasoning. But I didn't want to be stopped. Nicholas had his hands on my ass, and he was so very close to where I wanted him to go. All he had to do was move a little lower, his hands already pressing the cheeks of my ass apart, finger flirting between them, sliding up and down, further still until he grazed my wet folds and slipped in between them.

I strangled noise rose from my throat, filled with breathless need, and I looked at Joshua again. Still maintaining eye contact with Joshua, I let my legs fall further apart, giving Nicholas more room to slide a finger into my aching pussy. Then two, then three. I heard the metallic teeth of a zipper being pulled apart but I was still looking at Joshua. It wasn't him. It had to be Nicholas.

Yes. Nicholas. Give me what I need.

His fingers slid further inside, faster, stretching me as I begged silently for something else to fill me and give me release. All while maintaining eye contact with Joshua, who looked increasingly agitated. He stood, and walking over to the table where I lay, squirming under Nicholas's expert touch and said, "Roll over Elizabeth."

Absolutely.

Nicholas had to pull his hand away from me so I could roll over, and I mourned the loss of his touch. No sooner had I flipped on to my back though, then Joshua was on me, hands on my breasts, teeth grazing my nipples. My back arched off the table and I felt Nicholas's hands at my thighs, urging my legs apart. It wasn't until I felt the blunt head of his cock at my entrance that Joshua seemed to come to his senses.

"Nicholas, no."

"Nicholas, yes." I contradicted him. I was so filled with need after everything that happened already that day, no way was he going to deny me this. No way.

"That wasn't part of the agreement, you know that Nicholas."

"I didn't agree to shit," I panted. Angry now Nicholas hadn't said a thing, just hovered there, a condom already placed on his engorged cock. He stroked himself lightly, barely holding on to his self-control and. Well, fuck that.

"You two have been playing with me all day, and I don't want to be stopped by the only person in this room that has actually been allowed to get off. Nicholas wants to fuck me. I want him to fuck me. I would prefer he does it while you played with my tits, but if all you are going to do is complain then you can sit down on the couch and watch." I had no idea where those words came from, I had never said anything even remotely close to that in my whole life, and I would probably be mortified tomorrow. But today I was splitting open with need, and if Joshua was going to stand in my way, he could fuck right off. I was crazy with want, losing my mind from not being allowed satisfaction. Nicholas was panting heavily, watching Joshua, seeing what he would do. When Joshua didn't make a move to stop him, or sit down, Nicholas stroked his swollen dick and slid me a little further down the table.

Oh yes, this was happening.

"No," Joshua said loudly, damn close to yelling actually. "Don't do that. I have a better idea. Listen to me. Elizabeth, I'll give you something good. I'll give you both something good."

Both Nicholas and I looked at Joshua. He damned well better have something after being the cock blocker of the century.

"I'll take care of you, Elizabeth." He said, and his words washed over me like a caress. A promise.

"Why you?" Nicholas growled, angry at his prize being snatched away right before his eyes. "I want this, she wants this, so why you?"

"I'll take care of her," Joshua ground out, unbuckling his belt and letting his pants fall to the floor again. "I'll take care of her, and I'll take care of you. I'll give you my mouth," Joshua said to me, his eyes as dark as the ocean floor, "and I'll give you my ass." My mouth dropped open, and so did Nicholas's.

"You'd bottom for me? You've never bottomed for me." Nicholas breathed deep, nostrils flaring. He liked what Joshua was proposing that was for sure.

"It's been years since I've bottomed for anyone," Joshua admitted. "But now's the time so if we are going to do this, I suggest we get started. *He's* going to be here soon enough, and we need to be ready.

"Are you sure?" Nicholas asked, his hands trembling as he slid his jeans down the rest of the way. He was giving Joshua an out, but he was still getting ready.

Joshua turned all the way around, and grabbing Nicholas by the neck he claimed his mouth hungrily swallowing his doubt, dominating him completely Nicholas moaned into Joshua's mouth and I echoed the sound, completely undone by the display. "I trust you," Joshua said to Nicholas, before turning that hungry gaze to me. I was ready to weep I was so ready. I wanted someone, anyone to touch me, but I also wanted to see what they would show me.

Joshua slid the soft brown ottoman that I had placed beside the couch over to the end of the massage table, and gently knelt down on it, caressing my inner thighs with his hands as he did. My legs trembled as he spread them, letting his fingertips graze the wetness there, before placing a soft kiss on first one, then the other thigh until I was panting with need. Nicholas dripped some massage oil onto his hand and rubbed it all over his thick erection before doing the same thing over Joshua's ass, rubbing the oil down the crack before slipping one finger into his hole, all the way up to the knuckle.

Joshua moaned at the intrusion, and I mimicked him. I couldn't help it. Watching those two was just as erotic the second time around, only this time there were hands on my body as well. Hands hot as a branding iron as they spread my legs even further apart. "Spread yourself open for me," he murmured, and I slid my hands down to hold myself open, fully exposed. Joshua braced his arms on the massage table and bent his head low, so low I could sense his breath on my thighs. "Stop being so scared Nicholas. That's enough of your hand. Give me your cock. Fuck me like I know you've always wanted to because I'm going to eat Elizabeth like dessert." And then he put his mouth on me, and I screamed.

Joshua may have been bi, but he ate pussy like he had been training for a marathon. There was no way I was going to be able to last with those masterful strokes of his as he alternated between sucking my clit into his mouth and fucking me with his tongue. All the while moaning as his face was pushed deeper between my legs by Nicholas, who did not have to be told twice to get a move on. He'd slowly worked his whole length into Joshua, but once he was in, and Joshua's body had accepted the intrusion, all bets were off. "Oh God, I'm not going to last. Your ass is so tight, shit, Josh, hold still."

But Joshua wasn't holding still. He was forcing his ass back against Nicholas as he pushed into him, the rhythmic slapping of skin on skin bringing me to the point of frenzy. With every push Joshua rocked against me, his nose grazing my clit and his tongue working inside of me, mimicking what Nicholas was doing to him.

I came apart in a blistering orgasm, rocking against Joshua's face so hard it had to have hurt, but he didn't pull away. Just lifted his face to stare up the line of my body, eyes blasting a trail of heat while Nicholas continued to pound from the back. I might have wondered if Joshua was even enjoying himself, he made no noise, but his dick was an iron spike rising up between his legs and straining against his abdomen.

Nicholas made a strangled sound above him as Joseph reared back against him again. His breaths were coming closer and closer together, and still he kept up the rhythmic motion. "Come for me, Nicholas. Come for me while you fuck my ass." His dirty words may have been a turn on for me, but they worked magic for Nicholas, and he tensed up thrusting forward one last time before shouting his release to the ceiling. It took him a moment to pull out, like he was loathed to leave Joshua's body, but when he did Joshua turned around and kissed him. "I told you I would give you both something good," he said as he turned his cocky smile to me, proving that no matter what sexual position he was in, Joshua was definitely dominant.

I could only laugh weakly, barely having the strength to sit up on the massage table and swing my legs over the edge. My legs didn't want to hold me up though, and I stumbled a bit when I tried to stand. "Josh, why don't you take her to go clean up? I'll take care of things out here." Nicholas had already disposed of the condom he had used and was cleaning himself off with a wet wipe he had procured from somewhere. He must have seen the curious look on my face because he smiled wickedly and said, "I'm a masseuse, Elizabeth. Wet wipes in the travel bag are a must."

Should I have been more concerned about the lack of awkwardness in the aftermath of our sexscapade? Because there wasn't any. Joshua just led me to the bathroom where I was helped into the steaming hot shower. That I could do on my own, I didn't need any help. I also skipped washing my hair

considering I had already done that this morning
But, as Joshua urged from the other side of the
curtain where he used several washcloths to clean
himself, it was probably better I washed off the scent
of other men before *he* got here.

Whoever *he* was. This mystery man who was
going to show me what giving up control was. I probably should have been nervous, concerned, and
maybe even afraid. But all I could feel was relaxed,
sated, and satisfied. All of my frustration had disappeared, and I left the shower feeling completely
reborn – until I saw what was waiting on the bed
for me.

NINE

"WHAT IS THIS?" I came out of the bedroom, waving the tiny scraps of black cloth in my hand accusingly. "Am I supposed to put this on? I don't even know *how* to put this on." Nicholas was staring at the ceiling, trying very hard not to make eye contact and Joshua was fighting a smile. "Please tell me neither of you thinks I'm going to wear this."

"Oh no," Joshua said as he lost the battle and the smile stretched across his face. "I certainly did not pick it out, although I have to say I'm looking forward to seeing you in it."

"Nope. That is definitely *his* choice. *He* demanded we make sure you have it on when *he* gets here, actually."

"Nicholas, there are no bra cups." I turned my rage to him. "It's just elastic and lace. It's just lines.

My tits will be completely hanging out, what's the point?"

"Submission probably," Joshua said lazily from his seat on the couch while Nicholas packed up his bottles and gear and folded up his massage table. It made me sad to see him cleaning up. It meant that they were going to be leaving me soon.

"What do you mean by submission?" I asked, eyes narrowing. "I'm not into BDSM."

"You weren't into a ménage before earlier today I don't think either," Nicholas quipped, but then he saw my face and shut his lips.

"I don't think it's BDSM in this instance. Actually, I kind of understand after listening to him talk for a bit." Joshua sounded thoughtful as he scratched his chin and looked at me. "You have a serious control issue. It's getting to the point where you are working yourself into the ground. You had to take a couple of days off work in the middle of the week, didn't you? I was staying at the hotel for our LBBC conference over the weekend. I heard about the fight. Jesus, other people's children I tell you. Anyway, from what I understand, his purpose tonight is about getting you to let go of the need for constant control. And for that, you have to willingly let someone else have control over you. It's a trust thing. Just like I trusted Nicholas earlier today."

"I'm not doing butt stuff." I'd meant it as a joke. Sort of. I really wasn't going to do butt stuff.

Joshua and Nicholas said nothing, just looked at me patiently, waiting for me to come to terms with what Joshua had just said. "Ok, yes. I have a major control issue." I admitted with a frown. "But I don't see how me wearing scraps of nothing is fixing that particular problem."

Nicholas sighed and sat down next to Joshua on the couch, relaxing with one arm flung on the back of the cushions. "How about just doing what you are told without asking questions? See? Control issue."

Joshua's pocket started beeping and he pulled his phone out to check it. "Well guys, we have about twenty minutes to figure out if Elizabeth is wearing that...outfit...or not, because that is when *he* will be here."

Twenty minutes? And he was coming here? I don't know why I would have thought it was going to be anywhere else, but for some reason knowing there was a countdown had me nervous as hell. Sensing my nervousness the boys tried to calm me down.

"Easy Elizabeth," Nicholas said soothingly. "I've met the guy. I can vouch for him. You'll be okay."

"We won't leave you alone with him if you don't want. Remember, this is for you. No one can do anything to you that you don't want them to do. We'll make sure of it." Joshua stood and took the tiny scraps of black lace from my hand. "But I think you should open yourself up to this experience, I really do. You don't always have to be in control, Elizabeth. Let go and let someone else do the work." He grinned then, that charming and disarming smile and before I knew it, Joshua was leading me back to my bedroom and helping me into the series of tiny straps that made up the two-piece outfit. It was really nothing more than strappy black panties and cupless bralette with slits in the front where my nipples would poke out, but without someone to hold it correctly I would have never figured out how to put it on. I wondered if *he* knew that I would need help getting into it. I wondered if that was part of *his* plan.

"Oh shit, that's hot," Nicholas whistled as I walked back into the front room with Joshua. I wasn't embarrassed to be so exposed to these two. The stranger who was on his way to my house though, on his way to take control from me, that definitely had me shaking a little. I smiled weakly, shifting from foot to foot nervously. Ok, so I was wearing the ridiculous costume. What now? I saw Nicholas flick his gaze above my head to Joshua, before looking back, his face a mask of innocence. I whipped around just in time to see Joshua pull a length of black cloth out of his pocket and his eyes pleaded with me to understand.

"This next part is going to be a little more difficult to manage, Elizabeth, but trust me, it's going to be fine." I knew what he had in his hands, and no fucking way was he going to blindfold me.

"Um, what's next after that, boys? Does *he* want you to tie me to a chair?" Their guilty faces told me all I needed to know. "You are all out of your minds." Nicholas opened his mouth, but no words came out. Instead, there was a firm knocking on the door. Everyone froze.

No one made a move, even when the knocking sounded again. Ten more seconds passed by and then Joshua's pocket began to ring. "Hello?"

Joshua was silent for a moment as he listened to whatever was being said on the other side of the line. Then he sighed. "The outfit is on, but short of a wrestling match I don't think we are going to get the blindfold or the restraints on."

Restraints? I knew it.

"No one is tying me down, Joshua," I yelled across the room. "You can tell *him* that."

"Jesus, you can tell him yourself," and he gave me the phone, throwing his hands in the air, clearly giving up on the entire thing.

I grabbed the phone and snarled into it angrily "No one is tying me down, buddy."

"No one will do anything you don't want them to do." The voice on the other end of the phone startled me. I was expecting someone younger, like Joshua and Nicholas, but the voice on the other end of the phone was gravelly and deep. Smooth, but with rough edges. It was a strong voice. Too similar to someone else's for my liking and probably the beginning of my undoing.

"Then why are you trying to get Joshua to blindfold me and tie me to a chair?" I accused, angry, but also nervous. I was still in control. No one had done anything that I had said no to, so why was I shaking holding the phone?

"You need to stop trying to be in control of every little thing," the voice said. I had expected *him* to be harsh and unforgiving. Instead, this voice was easy, reasonable...familiar. "This is a lesson for you. A lesson in letting go. I can teach you how to do that - but you have to learn how to obey. And the best way to do that," he continued like he was explaining something incredibly simple to a small child, "is to remove your means with which to fight for that control. The restraints aren't necessary, and I'll gladly get rid of them if they make you uncomfortable. But the blindfold is non-negotiable." There was a hard edge to his voice now, and I can't say it was entirely unpleasant.

It was familiar somehow. Soothing.

"What happens if I say no to the blindfold too?" I was trying to be authoritative, but it came out as a breathy whisper, damn his voice and damn my imagination for running away from me.

"Absolutely nothing," he said. "I will turn around and walk away from here and you will not have to do another thing. But you'll wonder, what I would have done, what pleasure you could have had if you would have just let go of the reins for a short while. A simple 'no' from you will end everything. But it will end your entire contract. Your two young friends in there will be leaving with me as well, so please think carefully about your words. What do you really want? What are you willing to do? If you say no we all leave. But if you say yes, then I'm in charge. You answer to me." His sentence ended on a growl, and the sound of his voice was so familiar, I couldn't put my finger on it. Maybe it was just because it was through the phone but I couldn't help but think I had heard that voice before. I must have waited too long to answer because he prodded me again. "What is your answer? What do you want to do?" Instead of speaking I hung up the phone and handed it back to Joshua. I sat down on the ottoman that he had been kneeling on just a short while prior, took a deep breath and closed my eyes.

"No restraints. Just the blindfold. Hurry up before I change my mind." And as the cool black silk covered my eyes and Joshua tied it in a firm knot behind my head, I heard Nicholas open the door.

TEN

"WE HAD A FUCKING DEAL—WHY does it smell like sex in here?" He demanded before the door was even fully closed behind him. *Why was his voice so damn familiar?*

"Relax," I said dryly, "No one here broke any of your little rules. I heard about your gentleman's agreement."

"Elizabeth," Joshua nudged my side gently. Urging me to be quiet.

Footsteps came closer and then stopped in front of me. The silence went on so long I became nervous. I knew *he* was standing in front of me, but *he* wasn't saying anything. No one was. Finally, after what seemed like an eternity I felt a hand, a large hand fall gently on my naked shoulder. The hand didn't stay in one place though, it stroked gently down one arm and grazed the side of one breast lightly before settling on one knee. I felt him sink down to the floor in front of me. I couldn't see him but I could feel him there, sense the disturbance in the air.

"Oh my beautiful, proud princess," he murmured. "What are we going to do with that smart mouth?" His hands were massaging my knees and no matter how hard I willed them to stay closed out of spite, my traitorous body had other ideas. He carried the scent of spice and the outdoors. A scent that had always been so enticing to me because it reminded me of someone else. I knew this man could not be him because the other man was too nice, too easy going to carry out the role of dominant here, but I couldn't help but think about him anyway because that was who my imagination conjured up behind the blindfold. I saw who I wanted to see. I gripped the sides of the ottoman tightly as his hands massaged up the sides of my legs, the calluses on his fingers sliding roughly against my skin, sending delicious ribbons of pleasure zinging through me. This was a man who worked with his hands, I could tell.

I didn't want to like this strange man with his rough voice and his controlling demeanor, but my body had been wound so tightly all day that the slightest touch from him had me squirming in my seat. I could see nothing from behind the square of cloth covering my eyes, but the rest of my senses were on high alert.

"I'm sure you'll think of something," I said, more bravely than I felt. Desperate to maintain some sense of control, even as his hands urged my legs apart slightly, so he could lean in even closer to me. I don't know what I was expecting, but it certainly wasn't to be lifted straight off the ottoman and plopped down onto his lap. He'd lifted me up like I weighed nothing, and then occupied the space I had been seconds before, sitting me down on his lap like I was always meant to be there.

He wrapped his arms around my middle, and resting his chin on my shoulder, he said, "So tell me what you did today."

He had stubble, I could for sure tell because it scraped delicately across the skin of my shoulder and collarbone. I shivered at the sensation, my nipples tightening and poking out from between the slits in the ridiculous bra I was wearing completely against my will. I fidgeted in my seat, which happened to be a large man's lap. Much larger than Joshua or Nicholas. No, this man had legs like tree trunks, and he had no problem balancing me there while I squirmed in place. His large heavy hand was splayed out across my stomach, and I felt completely open and exposed as he nuzzled into the side of my neck. "Hmm? What did you do today?"

"Joshua made pasta mama and it was glorious. I feel asleep on the table during Nicholas's massage. It was nice."

I heard Nicholas snort at the "nice" comment but nothing I had said was false. We had a lovely lunch. I definitely fell asleep on the massage table. Other amazing things had happened too, but I was under no obligation to explain them to this man. I was fighting a battle of wills inside of myself. Curious about this man with the whiskey warm voice and his intentions, but reluctant to let go of the last shreds of my control. My stomach somersaulted as I was flipped over on my stomach, across his knees, and I heard more than felt his hand as he brought it down on my bottom once. It stung, but more than that it shocked me, and as I reared back in anger he was already rubbing circles over the hurt, soothing it with his large calloused hand. He dipped his fingers under the lace of that poor excuse for panties and massaged deeply, much like Nicholas had done earlier.

"Did you just spank me?" I shrieked. I was furious. I hated him. I hated myself for the dampness that was spreading between my legs at the feel of his hand on my ass. My temper may have said one thing, but my body couldn't lie. Damn it.

"You need to learn who is in control here, woman, and it isn't you. Now that didn't hurt, and you know it, but if you want to test my patience again I can give you another taste. Unless you like it when I smack your ass," he chuckled and I felt it reverberate through my body. "And if that's the case all you have to do is ask nicely and I'll crack your bottom again." He threatened, but his hand was still making lazy circles over my rear, his middle finger dipping briefly in between the cheeks with each pass. Not probing, just grazing. Taunting me. He was right. It hadn't hurt. But that didn't mean I wanted him to do it again.

Lie.

"Tell me the truth, did the boys put on a show for you?" He asked the question idly, but his hand was moving lower, down past my ass cheeks, coming dangerously close to finding that wet and aching part of me that still wanted to be filled. It was embarrassing, lying face down over this man's lap. But all I could focus on was the feel of his hand as it –

Crack.

The sting was harder this time, and just like before he immediately started rubbing the hurt away, this time his other hand reached under me to palm my breast. My nipples pebbled under his touch and he rolled one between his finger and thumb, having easy access through the slit in the bra I was wearing. I gasped, breathless with pleasure and surprise pain.

"What do you want from me?" I hated that I sounded like I was begging.

"I want you to let go." He commanded roughly. He sounded angry, like he was fighting a war. Neither of the boys was saying anything, and that made me nervous. Where they just watching me be humiliated? They had said they wouldn't let him do anything that I didn't want him to – they couldn't think that I wanted this treatment, could they?

"You said," I had to stop, tears clogged my throat and I had to start over. "You said you wouldn't do anything I didn't want you to do." My voice cut out and the last part ended in a whisper. Two tiny tears leaked out of the corners of my eyes, and instead of being absorbed by the silk they snuck through the sides of the blindfold and dripped down my cheek. I didn't want to cry. I was strong, in charge, and this was *my* fantasy. So why was I feeling so lost?

Someone must have moved then because I heard him bark out a pained 'no' and I wondered briefly why he sounded like he was hurting, when large hands gently lifted me back up. I was still on his lap though, and those thick arms wrapped around my middle again his hands rubbing lazy circles on my bare stomach. His scruffy chin nuzzled into my neck as he whispered to me.

"Oh Lizzie, it's not about what you want right now, it's about what you need."

His hands stilled and I gasped. I hadn't heard a word past the beginning of his sentence. *Lizzie*. Only one man had ever called me that and gotten away with it. Only one, and there could be no mistaking it this time. I wasn't hearing things. This wasn't my over heightened senses tricking me into hearing what I wanted to hear. Believing what I wanted to believe. This was *him*. He was *Blake*. I opened my mouth to call him out, reaching up to the blindfold covering my eyes intending to rip it off and confront him but he tightened his arms around my middle and spoke the next words directly into my skin.

"No. Don't do it. Don't say it. Don't break the spell, Lizzie. If you do it will be over, and I'll have to go. We need to do this. You need to do this."

Uncertainty bloomed in my stomach but my

heart beat double time and my breath was coming faster and faster. Instead of the sides of the ottoman my fingers gripped his thick thighs, digging in trying to steady myself, trying to get my mind right. This was *Blake*. This was *him*. It was one thing to think it in the recesses of my imagination, it was another thing to *know*. I could say what I wanted about needing to not be in charge, needing to be taken care of for just one day but this—this was my real fantasy. I'd never said his name in any of the questionnaires, but somehow Wesley had known? It didn't make sense, I didn't understand, but Blake was here, in my home. I was sitting on his lap in almost nothing at all, which he clearly enjoyed from the erection pressing against my lower back.

Blake.

Wanted me.

I'd thought him out of my reach but here he was, and suddenly the thought of giving up control didn't seem like something I should be fighting. If it was *him,* I could do it. If it was *him,* I wanted nothing more than to give myself up to whatever he wanted from me.

One of is large rough hands left my stomach and traveled down my thigh, resting on my knee. I couldn't control the moan that left my throat, nor the way my legs fell open, silently urging him to touch somewhere else. He squeezed the flesh of my leg, the softness of my inner thigh but moved no further to ease the furious ache that had become almost too painful to bear the moment I realized who held me in his arms.

"Please," I whispered, my head falling back against his shoulder, my body completely open to him. To take—whatever he wanted. Whatever he needed me to give. "Please." I had no control. I laid it firmly at his feet.

"I think it's okay now," I heard Nicholas speak from somewhere off to the side, close to the door. "I think she'll be fine with *him*. Joshua, let's give them some privacy." Privacy. Yes. Just Blake and me.

Letting him do whatever dirty things he wanted to do to me. I'd enjoyed my day, pushing sexual boundaries and breaking past self-imposed barriers. But Blake – he was different. I'd imagined him in my bed so many times, never thinking it would actually happen. I didn't want anyone else to see that, it was special, just for me.

Those arms held me still as first Joshua and then Nicholas kissed me on the forehead and said their goodbyes. A strangely jealous and intimate thing to do, considering they were leaving me with him. I wanted to be sad to see them go, I really did but all I could think was that I wanted the door shut and Blake to have his nasty way with me.

"I left you dinner in the fridge," Joshua whispered as he stroked my cheek with the back of his hand.

"I left our cards for you," Nicholas said, "you know, just in case you ever need our particular services again." The last part ended with a laugh as a throaty rumble shook against my back. Blake didn't like to think of me with these two. That was why the no penetration rule, and that was why he was growling noises of displeasure now. He was *possessive.* My fingers dug into his denim thighs. He still had me sitting on his lap, facing the room – but then the door clicked shut for the last time, and we were alone.

ELEVEN

BLAKE

I KNEW AS SOON as the door closed and those two cocky young upstarts left the apartment that I was in deep shit. I hadn't planned on her finding out it was me until much later in the evening. After dark actually, so I could throw her sunup to sundown rule right into a burning trash fire. Forget that not lifting a finger shit – this was my fantasy now and I needed her to use all of her fingers, preferably wrapping them around my dick.

But first we were dealing with a little trust issue, and I'll admit that was my fault considering I hadn't meant to fuck up and say her name like that. *Lizzie*. That was my name for her, and I'm the only man that says it – the only person actually. There was no damn way she could mistake my identity after that, and by the way all of the fight immediately left her body, I could only assume she was okay with it.

Well, I don't want to settle for her being just okay with me. That was the whole point of this exercise of this entire fucking day—to get her to want something so bad that she actually put forth some effort to get it. I was tired of tiptoeing around our mutual attraction. If she wouldn't acknowledge that she had feelings for me then I would make her, even if I had to make her uncomfortable in the process.

Still on my lap and facing the room I wrapped my arms around her waist again and kissed the skin over her left shoulder. "Lizzie. There's nobody here but you and me. What do you want to do?"

Step one. Throw her off guard.

Actually step one was to use those two young guys who *clearly could not follow directions* to gently coax her into bending a little bit. Get her open to the idea, get her motor running. I didn't expect them to flush her engine, and the thought of either one of them with their hands or mouths on her made me want to tie their necks together and kick them down a stairway. They were supposed to turn her on, not get her off—that was why we had the *no penetration* rule. The only one penetrating would be *me* Goddammit. I tightened my arms just to make sure she was still there, and I realized she still hadn't answered my question yet. She was just sitting still as a statue in my lap, trembling a little bit.

Trembling with desire would be okay, but I didn't want her shaking in fear. I didn't want to scare her—I wanted to motivate her. I waited long enough for her to come to understand what her body needed—me—but she was too determined to work her perfect round ass into early retirement to pay enough attention to what she really needed. Also me. But I wouldn't have her afraid. Fuck that.

"Lizzie. Talk to me." I licked my fingers and slid the wet pad of my thumb down her collarbone and into the lace of that worthless outfit I made her wear. Her nipples were so hard they burst through the material of the scandalous outfit I had prepared for her to wear. I didn't need to make her wear it—but I wanted her to give up a little bit more of that precious control she kept locked down. I wanted her to do something because I willed it. And now, looking at all of the soft luminous flesh laid bare to me—I was so fucking glad that I did. She arched into my hand, further proof that we were headed in the right direction and her fingers dug even harder into my thighs. I wonder if she even knew that she'd been creeping ever closer to my dick every time she grabbed a fistful of my jeans?

"I don't know what you want me to say…I just…I really want to look at you."

"Do you think you can handle that?" The original plan was to keep my identity a secret until she was so worked up she couldn't see straight anyway but that plan went to hell already so she might as well take it off.

"Am I still not allowed to say your name?" The words were whispered so softly, that if I hadn't been paying absolute attention to her, I might have missed them. I ran a fingertip down the front of her soaked and useless panties and she grabbed my hand holding it down, squeezing her legs tight over my fingers to keep them there a little longer.

My greedy little Lizzie. This was what I was looking for. I wanted her to need. I wanted her to want. I wanted her to *lust*. To know that she is not just a piece of the machine, working for someone else and running herself ragged. She was allowed to want and feel things.

I slid two fingers from my right hand under the small scrap of black satin and into her warmth. She opened her legs to ease my entrance and lifted her hips to invite me further as my left hand crept up to her breast and squeezed hard. Her entire body jerked and my dick leaped in response.

"You can say my name when you are coming all over my dick and not one minute before, Lizzie." I murmured into her ear as she squirmed, still pinned on my lap. "Can you handle that?"

"I just want to see you. Let me look at you." She was whimpering now, and the gentleman in me had to help ease her pain. The hand on her breast now moved to the blindfold, but the right hand kept busy sliding over her swollen clit, stopping to tap for a bit, pinching that little nub as she made breathless little sounds of pleasure. Even as I removed the blindfold from her eyes I kept my fingers in her pussy, listening as her breaths came faster and faster. I would make her come before she saw my face for sure.

My dick swelled to painful proportions underneath the curve of her ass as she dug her heels into the floor and pushed back against me, coming apart on my hand. I didn't know how long I would be able to continue the farce of having iron control. I needed to get inside her. I needed to fuck her. I'd been patient for so long—waiting for her to get over whatever personal hang-ups she had about dating a coworker. I knew she was interested. I could tell by the way she watched me and the way a blush stained her cheeks every time I said something with double meaning. Which I did—often and on purpose. I didn't realize how tightly wound she was at first. I kept thinking she would come around in time. But she didn't. And I'd spent long enough jerking off in my fist, waiting for her to get with the program.

It was me who'd first approached Wesley about giving the LBBC card to Elizabeth. It was me who arranged the entire thing with the Little Black Book Club. And as soon as she went to the website and answered all of the questions I knew – she was mine.

And now I was about to have her.

I let her catch her breath, but as soon as I noticed she was coming down from the high of her quick orgasm I took advantage and twisted her around in my lap. Turning her to face me, with her knees straddling my lap I looked into her soft grey eyes, pupils wide and unfocused.

"Hello." I smiled at her then, my normal, charming, everyday smile. Then I kissed her. Slowly sweeping my tongue across the inside of her mouth feeling her open up to me little by little until I felt her tongue reach out and tangle with mine. She was still a little too hesitant for my liking.

"You wouldn't happen to be a virgin, would you,

Lizzie?" That earned me a disgruntled look and a frown.

"No. I just don't know what I am supposed to be doing right now." Looking down at my chest, probably so she wouldn't have to be looking into my eyes anymore, she picked nervously at the buttons of my shirt. "I know the LBBC is all about fantasy, and I did sign up for the program, but I never dreamed they would be able to tell. That they would *know*..."

This was interesting. Now we were getting somewhere. "What did they know?" I asked, tilting her face back up so she was looking at me again. "Tell me." I leaned in to kiss her again before moving both hands to the straps of the open cup bra she was wearing, sliding them down her shoulders and peeling the entire thing off until she was completely exposed to me. Her tits were pale but her nipples were a deep rosy pink and thrusting forward fiercely. I cupped the fullness of her breasts in both hands, rubbing my thumbs across her tight buds until she shuddered and leaned into my touch.

"I always wondered what it would feel like if you touched me." She admitted shyly. Shy. That was uncharacteristic for my Liz. She was normally in command of every situation.

"Do you want to find out what I feel like inside

you?" Her pupils dilated while I watched. She mos*
certainly fucking did.

"Yes."

"Then tell me. This is your chance. Say th*
words. Don't just nod or do what you think I wan*
you to do. Tell me what *you* want." *Please don't leav*
me hanging,* I thought to myself as I bounced her *
little in my lap so I could adjust my dick. She wa*
taking a long time with her reply. Every second o*
silence a painful, excruciating wait.

"But..." *No buts Lizzie. Fuck me, no buts.* "But *
have to go back to work in two days. What are we
going to do then?"

Are you fucking kidding me right now, woman?

"Elizabeth." I said sternly. Her whole name thi*
time and her head snapped up in surprise, al*
pretense of shyness gone. I pinned her with a*
angry scowl. "I cannot believe," I growled angrily*
"that you are thinking about work right now. A plac*
that neither of us has to be for two more fuckin*
days. When I am sitting here, just waiting for you t*
give me the words I need to bend you over ever*
piece of furniture in this room. Consent Lizzie*
That's what I'm asking for. Your body has alread*
told me you're ready, I can feel how hot you are righ*
through my pants – but I don't want you to *just g*

along with it. I'm waiting for you to tell. Me. What. You. Want."

She shifted in my lap then, just a twitch of her ass, but she ground against me in such a way that I couldn't help but groan and close my eyes. She was killing me. I was going to die today with a hard on— so close to victory. She must have made some kind of decision then, while I was groaning in pleasure-pain, because when I opened my eyes she was smiling at me.

"So much talking. Aren't there other things you want to be doing than talking?" *Yes, that's what I've been waiting for, thank you for noticing.* "It's not that I don't want, because I do—and have—for so long." Her hands had stopped plucking at the fabric of my shirt and began slipping the buttons through the holes, spreading the opening wide so she could slide her hands against the bare skin of my chest. "It's just that I feel like this is a dream. I'm afraid I'm going to wake up and you won't be here. That I made this up inside my head."

I grabbed one of her hands and pressed it at the place our bodies met, lifting my hips up to meet her. "Do I feel like a dream?"

Her soft gray eyes deepened into storm clouds and I could see the exact moment she gave herself up to the experience. "Take me to the bedroom," she whispered, and I smiled again. This time it wasn't a friendly smile. I was a predator. She was prey.

"Lizzie. Bedrooms are for sleeping. I don't know about you but I'm not in the least bit tired. What I want," I said as I slid her off of my lap and onto the cushion next to me, laying her back so I could lean over her, my forearms resting on either side of her body. "What I want is to take you on every surface in this room. I want to fuck you so hard, and so much that you can't even sit down and watch television without thinking of my cock inside of you. So that, in two days when we both have to go back to work, you can't walk past my office without getting wet. And since I know you are worried what is going to happen in the future I will let you in on a little secret. This is just the beginning. I finally have you and I'm not letting go, so forget about things ending when the day is over. This isn't your fantasy anymore, it's mine. And mine doesn't have a time limit." I stood up then, looking down at the line of her body as she lay propped up against the cream colored cushions of her overstuffed sectional. I slid the shirt she had already unbuttoned for me down and off my shoulders, letting it fall soundlessly to the floor. Reaching for the snap on my jeans I flicked it open with my thumb, and slowly pulling the zipper down I said the last thing I was going to on the subject. "I think we've done enough talking, Lizzie. I'm going to fuck you now."

Dirty talking makes Lizzie hot.

I would have to remember that little nugget of wisdom because she was on me in a hot second, galvanized into action with her hands on mine before I could even slide my jeans off my hips. "Let me," she whispered as she pushed my pants down and her busy fingers slid me out of my boxers, exposing my hard length. Tiny drops of wetness already glistened at the tip, I'd been waiting for this for so long already. Feeling her hands on me was almost too much, and I thrust my hips forward without thinking about it, my body already wanting more of her.

"Oh, God, yes. Just let me, just for a minute..." she said, and she took me into her mouth. All the way in one shot. No gentle touches, no soft licking, she just gobbled straight down like she was starving and took my cock deep into her throat, forcing me past the tight circle of her lips and sucking in her cheeks.

Shit. Fuck. All of the control I had been exercising flew away in a puff of air and I could only grab onto her head, mostly to keep myself steady, as she slid her mouth up and down on my cock. When her hand reached up to fondle my balls it was almost my undoing. *Too good. I won't last.* Even my internal thoughts were choppy and vague, but I knew that if I didn't pull her face off my dick soon I would be shooting straight into her mouth. And while that visual did all sorts of things to for my erection, it wasn't how I wanted to begin the evening with Lizzie. Blow jobs were great, but I wanted to fuck her. I wanted to brand her.

I wanted to make her mine.

But she wouldn't stop. Not when I tugged on her hair, not when I started to pant and not even when I begged her, "Lizzie, please stop. I'm going to come." She just moaned and sucked harder, like she was willing me to go, desperate to swallow my entire load. *Christ Lizzie.* I wanted to let her, and there would be time for this kind of playing later. But this first time – this first time had to be different, and I had to pull myself away from her a little roughly to disconnect. For me anyway. She just looked up at me, a small frown on her face.

"I wasn't ready yet." She complained, and dared to reach up and pinch my butt cheek.

"Woman, get your ass on the couch." I hadn't

meant to roar, but she had pushed me almost past my limit, and I was scrambling to maintain some sense of control. Over her. Over myself. Over the whole damned situation.

She stood up, slowly, probably wondering what I was going to do. I turned her by her shoulders and gave her a little shove. "On your knees," I barked roughly, mostly because I wanted her so badly I could barely speak and I needed her to move a little faster. "Face the couch and lift your ass for me Lizzie, it's punishment time."

"What kind of punishment?" She asked nervously, but she did as I instructed, knees on the seat cushions, legs wide and arms braced against the back of the couch. She didn't fool me. She wanted whatever I was going to dish out to her, and there was no way I could mistake the trembling in her body for fear now. She wanted me, and she was going to get as much of me as she could take.

She waited there, looking over her shoulder while I reached into my pants pocket and pulled out a condom. I rolled it on slowly, not to torture her, but to give myself a moment to get under control. She was the one who was supposed to be losing it, not me. Damn how those tables had turned so quickly. With the condom on, and a firmer grasp of my libido

I ran my hand over the soft curve of her ass, and then gave it a swift slap. She cried out, but didn't try to move away. In fact, she lifted her ass a bit higher in the air instead, and I rubbed away the sting before sliding my hand further down to test her wetness.

"Please," she moaned, burying her face in the soft fluffy cushions she was leaning against.

"Please what, Lizzie? You've gotten so greedy, just what is it that you want?"

"Please," she said again, but a little louder this time as she bumped her ass against my waiting erection, "I want you inside of me. Fill me up."

She didn't have to tell me twice.

She was so wet, there was zero resistance as I slid inside of her, entering her so hard my balls slapped against her thighs. For a second I couldn't move, if I did I would blow so I grabbed both sides of her ass and held her there, not moving. She pushed against me, low noises of pleasure moving up her throat and past her lips.

"I want to move." She pushed against me again and that delicious friction was enough to snap the tenuous grasp I had and I surged into her hard pushing her deeper into the cushions, making her cry out.

"Are you that hungry for my cock, Lizzie?" I

asked, knowing that my filthy words would only serve to push her closer to the edge. "Then take it. Take all of me my dirty girl, take everything I give you." And then I gave her exactly what she wanted. Hard strokes. Punishing strokes. The sound of our bodies crashing together ricocheted off the walls in the otherwise silent apartment. The only other noise was the sound of our harsh breathing, my grunts of pleasure and Lizzie's gasping breath.

I knew the exact moment when things changed. When they hit the point of no return and Lizzie started tightening around me. Her body milking me as she entered the upward climb towards orgasm and she said the one thing she wasn't supposed to say. The one thing that shredded the remnants of my control and caused fireworks to explode behind my eyes.

My name. She screamed my name.

"Blake," she wailed as her orgasm swept her up and away. "I'm coming Blake, fuck me harder. Harder."

And I did. Slamming into her, forcing her down until I was drilling her mercilessly into the couch. Until the aftershocks calmed and both of us collapsed into a pile of arms and legs on the cushions. Somehow she had twisted onto her back and I ended up on top of her, chest to chest, my face buried in her neck. It was becoming one of my favorite places to be.

I also knew the moment she realized what she had done because her entire body froze. Before I could even speak a word to calm her, she wrapped both arms around my neck and squeezed.

"Don't go."

Who was going anywhere? Not me, that was for damn sure.

"Don't go. I know I wasn't supposed to say it, but I couldn't help it. Don't leave me yet. Don't go. Please."

Oh, my sweet girl. "Lizzie, I said as I loosened the choke hold she had on me. "You couldn't get rid of me right now if you tried. "And I think, if you are going to scream anyone's name as you come, mine should be the only one on your lips."

"Blake," she said again, less hesitantly this time. "What are we even doing right now?"

"Right now? Well, right now I think we should clean up. Then I think we should look in the fridge and see what punk number one left for us to eat. Then after that I thought we could take a shower together. And by shower I obviously mean *shower sex*, and then—"

"Okay, that' not what I meant and you know it,"

Lizzie said, laughing. She looked up at me with her grey eyes wide and trusting. "What are we doing right now? How did we get here?"

I knew I'd have to tell her, I guess now was as good a time as any. I really didn't want to do it with the condom still hanging on my dick so I excused myself to the restroom to get a quick clean up. Coming back from the bathroom with a warm wet washcloth I bent low in front of Lizzie, who was still sitting on the couch. She reached for the washcloth but I ignored her hands, and kneeling down I went to work, rubbing the cloth over her thighs and her sex in lazy circles. Cleaning her up but taking my time doing so.

"I'm the reason you met Wesley." Her eyes grew even bigger as she registered my statement.

"You stopped the elevator on purpose?"

"What? No. Although that was kind of a bonus. He was supposed to approach you at some point over the weekend. The elevator situation just kind of fell into our lap. Only time I've been grateful for that piece of shit elevator." I grumbled. This sounded better when I was trying to explain it in my head.

"I don't understand, you wanted me to act out my fantasy? I still don't know how you knew it involved

you." Hearing Lizzie say out loud that I was a part o
her fantasy had my dick swelling to attention again.

"Not exactly. Actually, you aren't the client, I am."

Nothing. Radio silence. The only indication I
had that she heard my words was the scarlet blush
staining her cheeks. I forged ahead. "I've been trying
to get you to notice me for the longest time. To see
me as a man, and not just a coworker, and I was
pretty sure there was an attraction there. But Lizzie
you are so high strung. Everything is work, work
work, you never relax. Even when I point blank tell
you to relax – you blow it off. You were never going
to let me in. You were too rigid. Too disciplined."

Lizzie blinked at me, clearly trying to process the
information.

"But why the LBBC? Why didn't you just ask
me out?"

"Lizzie I have asked you out eight times in the
last two years. Every time you laugh and blow me
off. If it wasn't for your eyes on my crotch every time
I walked by you, I would assume that you didn't like
me and leave it at that. But I could see in your face
and your body language that you did. You wanted
me and I knew it. I just wish you would *say*
something."

She reached up and placed the palm of her hand

against the side of my face, and I rubbed my stubble against her skin, tickling her. "It wasn't that I didn't like you, Blake," she said with a sign. "The problem is that everyone likes you. *Everyone*. How could I take you seriously when you act that way with every person you come across? You are everyone's favorite person, Blake. How could I assume that I was special compared to anyone else?"

That pissed me off.

"Have you ever seen me with another woman?" I growled, pinned her with my stare. "Have you ever heard me asking another woman out for drinks, for dinner, for anything? This is exactly why I signed up with Little Black Book Club. I needed help, and you needed an excuse. An outlet. A reason to give up your iron control over everything in your life. I knew that if you took that card and got curious enough, you would look up the website. And I also knew, that if you filled out the fifty pages of questions," she laughed then. I knew it was a lot, I had filled it out too. "I knew that if you did all of that then you were at least open to the idea. We both wanted it, Lizzie. You just needed to say yes."

There it was. I'd laid the whole story out on the table for her to either accept, or deny me. I hoped that she would accept me, and the lengths that I had gone through to get her to understand my feelings, but even I knew that was a stretch. It was a sexy scheme on paper, but she would be well within her rights to be incredibly freaked out by what we had done. For the first time since I had asked for Wesley's help, I felt nervous. What if she told me to leave? What if she decided she couldn't work with me anymore?

I squeezed my eyes shut briefly to quell those doubtful feelings. I had just been inside of her. It was my name she had screamed on the breath of her release. She wanted me just as badly as I wanted her and from the way she was running her fingertips up and down my arm, I didn't think she would be shoving me out the door anytime soon. Opening my eyes, I met her soft gray stare.

"I'm hungry." That was it. It was almost like she completely dismissed everything I had just told her.

"You're hungry?" I knew Joshua had left dinner in the fridge. After almost breaking the rules earlier, and even though they didn't say anything I could tell by how disheveled everyone was that *something* had happened, he had better have done his *actual* job.

Lizzie bit her lip, her hand running down my arm moved lower, and then lower still. She found me, still semi-hard and poking against her leg, and stroked me gently. My cock swelled in her hand, never mind the normal recovery time, I was ready to go again and I thrust into her hand, willing her to continue.

"You didn't let me finish earlier," her tongue darted out and she licked her lips slowly. "I'm still hungry."

Oh, I knew what she meant. Hungry. For me. Well if my lady wanted something, all she had to do was ask and I would provide. All uncertainty passed, we were on the same page now, and I didn't have to worry about what would happen if she denied me. We were past that now.

"Let's go to the bedroom then, and I'll feed you properly." The couch had sounded like a good idea when we were both blinded by lust, but a big soft bed would be much more comfortable.

"I thought you said the bedroom was just for sleeping?" She looked at me, her eyes wide with confusion as I scooped her up in my arms and strode down the hall.

"Well yeah," I winked and gave her my cockiest grin. "We'll get to sleep. Eventually."

ABOUT THE AUTHOR

Remi is the author of the Little Black Book Club Series and writes steamy, toe-curling-look behind you to see if anyone is reading over your shoulder-erotic romance. When not writing Remi is usually reading, crafting, or running incredibly short distances at an unreasonably slow pace.

Follow Remi on Facebook at
www.facebook.com/RemiRichland

Join Remi's mailing list for new content and exclusive giveaways at www.remirichland.com

Read the next book in The Little Black Book Club - VANILLA

Coming Soon - OVERNIGHTER

Other Books by Remi Richland

Gray Area - An erotic menage short story

Sign up for my newsletter HERE

Follow me on Facebook HERE

.

Made in the USA
Middletown, DE
12 August 2019